Anna Chapin Ray

Each Life Unfulfilled

Anna Chapin Ray

Each Life Unfulfilled

ISBN/EAN: 9783337095819

Printed in Europe, USA, Canada, Australia, Japan

Cover: Foto ©Andreas Hilbeck / pixelio.de

More available books at **www.hansebooks.com**

EACH LIFE UNFULFILLED

BY

ANNA CHAPIN RAY

AUTHOR OF "TEDDY, HER BOOK," ETC.

BOSTON

LITTLE, BROWN, AND COMPANY

1899

University Press

JOHN WILSON AND SON, CAMBRIDGE, U.S.A.

Each Life Unfulfilled

CHAPTER ONE

"REALLY, Mr. Heaton, I can't see what ever brought you to this wilderness."

"Really, Miss Tiemann, the same remark might apply to you."

The girl laughed lightly.

"To me? Oh, the farm is a regular feature of my summer existence. For the past seven years we have spent July here, and I shall probably go on spending July in this hamlet till the end of time. Auntie always rushes off, directly after Commencement, to get rested from her mad whirl of gayety."

"Commencement?"

"Yes; my uncle is president of one of these microscopic western colleges. You see, I know how you Harvard men regard us. But you have n't answered my question."

"As to what?"

"How you chanced to come here into that camp." There was a slight, a very slight accent of scorn in her voice.

"Oh, 't was one of Jack's flights. We are off for the summer, and somebody in Chicago told him of the place. It sounded promising, so he drifted up here to see what it was like."

"And you drifted with him. You must be an ideal companion, Mr. Heaton, to follow your leader so blindly."

Heaton dropped his oars for an instant, and pushed back his little gray cap.

"Why not?" he answered. "The trip was of Jack's making. I had no plans to speak of, only to get off and take a long vacation while I was free to go."

"I'm going to ask another question," she announced, after a brief interval. "Right oar, please! I hate to give orders in this peremptory fashion; but you are running us straight into the other boat. Who is Jack?"

"Did n't you see him? Oh, no; I remember. He had gone before I met you. He is a young cousin of mine, a fine fellow, too; going to be a doctor as soon as he has cut a few more wisdom teeth and attended a few more clinics. He went up, Tuesday morning, to spend a week with some friends in Waukesha; but I did n't care anything about the people, so I preferred to stay here and wait for him. It's so like Jack to go rushing off at a moment's notice."

He had taken up his oars again, and his companion was silent for a time, as she sat

2

watching the steady, strong sweep of the blades through the water, and the slender, sinewy hands of the man before her. She liked his hands, for they were slim, but firm. All in all, she liked his whole appearance, and she looked at him more closely than she had done at all since she had met him, two days before. He was tall and slight and alert, yet with a little air of hesitancy at times, which she was at a loss to explain. His voice was distinct, but low and quiet, and his manner impressed her as being an odd blending of strength and gentleness.

"How do you like the camp?" she resumed, after a prolonged pause.

Heaton looked up at her, with a sudden flash of fun in his brown eyes.

"Immensely, in my own way. It's a little different from anything I have seen, and I've enjoyed sitting back and watching the others. Jack is in the middle of it all; but I couldn't quite stand that, and it was growing rather monotonous, so I was glad enough when old Napoleon, as the boys call him, took it upon himself to introduce me to your aunt, the other day."

"Auntie hailed you at once as a congenial spirit," Miss Tiemann answered, as she trailed her little brown hand through the baby waves that were following their boat. "She came back to the house, rapturous because you had

3

agreed to carry her letters to the post office. If you ever want to win Auntie's heart, just help her to get, or to send off her mail, and in return she will grant you the half of her kingdom."

"Then row over to the village with me, Monday afternoon, and bring back the mail," he returned quickly. "I often go up, and her letters will give me an additional excuse, you know."

"Left oar, quick!" was the sudden response. "You are running right into those lily pads. I can't talk and steer this rudderless boat at the same time, without wrecking both ourselves and the conversation. It is too quiet and pretty to talk, anyway."

"But will you go?" he urged.

"Yes, anywhere, so long as I can be on this charming little lake. Auntie won't let me go out alone, and there isn't anybody here—" She paused abruptly, fearful of having given too broad a hint.

"You are forgetting Father Napoleon," he said gravely. "Still, I shall be very grateful if you will let me take you out often, as long as we stay. It's a bit lonely for me here, since Jack went."

"I shall probably be the one to go first," she replied; "for we leave here, next Thursday."

"So soon as that? I'm sorry."

"So am I, for I love the place, in spite of the

4

six o'clock breakfasts at the farm; but Auntie has other engagements for August, and I usually follow her as dutifully as you do your cousin."

She was silent again, and sat leaning back in her place at the stern, with her eyes fixed on the distant outline of the hotel on the hillside above the lake. Heaton looked at her stealthily, from moment to moment, and he was conscious of a greater sense of enjoyment than he had experienced before since Jack had left him. In fact, he had missed his cousin sorely, though he had urged his going away for a week's break in their continual intercourse. Jack's bright, happy-go-lucky fashion of floundering along through life made him the best possible companion that Heaton could have had just then; and, notwithstanding his occasional moody days, he was thoroughly grateful for his cousin's jovial willingness to give up his other plans and spend the summer killing time with him in out-of-the-way corners of the earth. To be sure, it was Heaton who paid all the bills; but, on the other hand, Jack was giving him more than mere money could ever buy.

The people at the camp had not interested him in the least. Their jokes passed his comprehension, and their free-and-easy intercourse grated on his sensibilities. Neither had he cared, till now, to go over to the hotel, two miles away. He was usually to be seen paddling about on the lake, or lying in his hammock, or else seated cross-legged beside his tent, writing page after page with an eagerness which had led the jocose Napoleon to circulate the report that he was penning endless love letters.

He was certainly lonely, and he had gladly seized his opportunity, two days before, when Napoleon had waylaid him with the information that Mrs. Mackie was hunting for some one to carry her letters across the lake. Heaton knew Mrs. Mackie by sight. The little gray-haired woman and her pretty niece were familiar figures about the camp, and he had willingly placed himself and his boat at her service. His zeal had been rewarded. He had brought back a goodly handful of letters which he had delivered at the farm, and Mrs. Mackie, effusive in her gratitude, had introduced him to her niece and left the girl to entertain him while she lost herself in the mazes of her correspondence.

In the easy, off-hand life at Idlewilde, acquaintances were quickly made, and it had seemed quite natural, when Saturday night came, that Heaton should offer to row Miss Tiemann up to the hotel, for the weekly hop. The boat from the farm was already full, and Mrs. Mackie had easily fallen in with the young man's suggestion. She had implicit belief in her womanly intuitions, and from the moment of her meeting him, she had been convinced that she could safely trust

Mr. Heaton in all things, even with her care-fully-guarded niece.

Heaton was glad now that he had decided to risk the proposition, even though it had taken him out of his self-sought quiet, and had cost him some grumbling at the narrow limits of his tent mirror. Full dress might be undesirable; but at least he did like his tie to be smooth, and even this was difficult to attain before a glass five inches long.

The summer twilight was darkening the upper end of the lake; but at the west there still lingered a rosy glow. He watched the girl, as she sat outlined against it, with one hand holding the folds of her dainty summer gown, the other negligently dangling in the water beside the boat, while her pretty, girlish face was raised to look at the stars coming out in the velvety blue above her head. He could study her at his ease, for she had given herself up to a rapt, childlike enjoyment of her surroundings, and was quite unconscious of his gaze. She was so young, so pretty with the rosy light falling across her face and deepening the tones of her pale pink gown! In after years he never quite lost the memory of the picture before him during their first hour alone together.

The other boat came alongside, as they bumped against the piles at the landing, and Miss Tiemann roused herself from her reverie.

A moment later, she was laughing and chattering with the friends who had rushed down from the hotel to meet her at the landing. It was plain that she was a general favorite; but although she was the central figure of the enlarged group, she kept Heaton close at her side, as they scrambled up the steep hill and entered the great dining-room, already cleared for dancing. Here Heaton was forced to abandon her to the others for a time; and, not caring to dance with any one else, he attached himself to Mrs. Mackie's side, where he sat talking dutifully to her while his eyes followed her niece, as she whirled past him. She danced, as she did everything else, with a frank enjoyment which made it seem impossible that she would ever pause or grow weary. Heaton, though he had supposed his dancing days were ended, grew restless and heedless of Mrs. Mackie's friendly commonplaces while he waited for his own turn to come.

Nevertheless, the pleasantest time of all was when he was rowing them both, aunt and niece, homeward under the quiet light of the stars. They talked fitfully, now discussing some trivial event of the evening, now lapsing into a silence only broken by the regular plash of the oars, as they struck the smooth surface of the lake. The other boat had lagged far behind, out of sight and hearing, and the world about them was very still. All at once Miss Tiemann began to sing to herself with the little, low, humming sound of a contented child.

"Sing something, Elinor," her aunt urged.

"Please do," added Heaton, turning to look around at her, as she sat behind him in the bow of the boat.

"Too bad of you, Auntie, to disturb my dreaming! Truly, Mr. Heaton, I don't sing very much; it's only a fond aunt's partiality that makes her ask me."

"Let me be the judge of that," he insisted.

Without more ado, she began to sing a little Slumber Song of Kücken, simple and quaint, but well suited to her clear, light soprano voice. She showed training and accuracy, yet her voice lacked something which perhaps time alone could give. Nevertheless Heaton, as he listened to her and unconsciously adapted his stroke to the rhythm of her song, was supremely content. He wished that Jack were there to accompany her with his rich tenor. Then, upon reflection, he was devoutly thankful that Jack was several miles away, doubtless paying court to some other fair maiden. Jack usually had all the women at his feet; for once it was better to have him at a safe distance.

CHAPTER TWO

"PROMPT to the minute!" Elinor exclaimed gayly, as she came running down to the landing, two days later.

Heaton held up his watch.

"I was n't going to tell you," he said, laughing; "but you boasted too much, and your pride must be humbled. You are exactly five minutes behind time."

"I could n't help it," she returned impenitently, as she took his outstretched hand to steady herself on the way to her seat. "I've been in a state of persecution, this last hour, and I could n't escape before."

"Who has been persecuting you?" he asked, while he let his oar-blades drop into the water.

"The minister here. He wanted me to sing at a concert, next week. I believe it was for the benefit of the Sunday-school melodeon; but I 'm not sure. Anyway, he asked me if I could n't sing ' Silver Threads among the Gold.' Fancy it!" And she laughed gleefully to herself.

"Might I inquire what answer you gave?"

"I showed unbounded tact. I told him that I 'd heard it and it was a sweet thing, a very sweet thing, but I was afraid I could n't sing it. Besides, I was going away too soon. He offered to change the date; but of course I could n't allow that."

"Miss Tiemann, how long since you finished your studies at the Jesuit college, over here?"

"I came from there yesterday, and left the fathers all bemoaning my departure," she replied demurely. "But I was quite sincere. It's a song that I 've often heard alluded to as being ' real pretty.' To be sure, one man I met applied the same words to the ' Messiah ' *Hallelujah*. He meant well; but his language struck me as being a trifle inadequate."

"Are you working much at your music?" Heaton asked, as he pointed the boat's bow up the lake and dropped into his usual slow, steady stroke.

Averse as she generally was to speaking of her plans, Miss Tiemann felt no reserve, as she met the friendly eyes that were looking into her own. There was no tinge of self-assertion in Heaton's manner, yet she was conscious of feeling very young and childish beside him, and it was with the simplicity of a child that she answered his question.

"For two years I have given all my time to it, nearly. I want so much to be able to sing well, some day; but I am afraid there is n't much chance for it."

11

In spite of himself, Heaton smiled at the sudden note of despondency in her tone.

"One of my good friends has said, 'If you must, you must, and many musts will make a hit,'" he observed. "You'll probably get your success, if you work for it. Most people do in this world, I notice. Where have you studied?"

"Only at home as yet; at home with Auntie, that is. My home has been with her since my father and mother died."

"So your parents are dead, too," he said quickly, as if pleased at discovering this bond of sympathy. "I'm alone, too, so I live with my married sister in New York, when I'm at home."

"Where does your cousin live?" questioned the girl idly, more from a desire to get away from the subject of her singing than because she felt any especial interest in the reply.

"New York, too. We've grown up together ever since we were small boys, and we are great chums, even if he is five years younger than I."

"By the way," remarked Miss Tiemann; "Auntie was asking why you didn't come over to see us, last night."

"I wasn't invited," Heaton responded; "and I didn't know how strictly you might be keeping Sunday."

"We take a vacation here," she answered, as

she raised her sun umbrella and held it, sail-wise, to catch the fresh breeze. "There, is n't that a help?"

"Yes, only I 'm afraid you will be burnt to a cinder without it."

She glanced upward at the blazing sun.

"I don't care," she returned. "I 'm in a mood to defy Auntie to-day. She wails bitterly over my copper-colored nose, and I actually think she 'd insist on my wearing one of those floppy sunbonnets, like the women in camp, if I were only a little younger and more biddable."

"After all, sunburn is fashionable," said Heaton consolingly, though the dazzling glare on the water was reddening his own cheeks and narrowing his eyes to a pronounced squint.

"That 's what they all say; but, if the truth were known, there 's a great deal of nonsense written about the summer girl and sunburn. They say we sit by the summer sea, and read Arnold and Clough and those men; but that 's all they know about it. What we girls really do, when we 're socially off duty, is to wrestle with the sunburn on our noses, and rue the day we were enticed into going crabbing."

"I hope your Sunday was successful."

"How unkind of you to twist my words so! Up here, I don't mind, and I grow red and brown till Auntie holds up her decorous hands in horror."

If the darkness had made Miss Tiemann dreamy, the other night, the sunshine appeared to be producing the reverse effect to-day, and she chattered constantly while the boat danced along over the water. Heaton answered to her mood until his face lost something of its quiet gravity and grew suddenly young and boyish. There was something indescribably attractive to him in this pretty little maiden with her wavy brown hair and her bright brown eyes. Her saucy fun and her evident enjoyment of each passing moment reminded him of Jack; but, in spite of her twenty years and a certain womanly trimness of her slight figure, she seemed to him years younger than his tall cousin.

In reality, Heaton was several years her senior; but the apparent difference between them was far greater than the actual, for as a rule he talked little, and his manner was as quiet and settled as hers was buoyant. Moreover, at times a close observer might have noticed a little look of weariness about his kind brown eyes, and the short brown mustache that shaded his upper lip could not quite conceal the lines which time, or care, or sorrow had traced about his sensitive mouth. He was in no sense a handsome man; but, in looking into his thin, clear-cut face, one instinctively realized that he was of good material and finely wrought, and he wore his rough-and-ready camping suit with an ease which showed that his tailor respected him more than he respected his tailor.

Elinor came out from the little post office with her arms full of letters and packages.

"No," she answered to Heaton's offer to relieve her of her burden; "I am going to carry them back to the boat. It makes me feel rich to be holding so many letters, even if they are n't all for me. We'll divide when we get into the boat; till then, you must possess your soul in patience."

"Very well." And Heaton took her umbrella. "If you wish to turn postman, you are welcome; but at least you will let me save your long-suffering cheeks one bit of friction."

"Oh, no; let me have the sun, please," she begged. "It is too late for it to do me any harm now, and it is almost my last chance, we are going away so soon. I'm a real child of the country, for I love the fresh air and the sunshine and this wonderful clear light on the hills."

Heaton's brows contracted.

"So do I," he muttered, half to himself.

Seated in the boat, Elinor fell to sorting the letters in her lap.

"Mrs. Mackie, Mrs. Mackie, Mrs. Mackie, Mr. T. M. Heaton," she read. "Mrs. Mackie, Mr. Thomas Murray Heaton —" She raised her eyes abruptly.

Heaton was watching her, while an amused

little smile played about the corners of his mouth.

" Well? " he asked.

" Is that your name? " she demanded.

" It certainly is."

" Are there two of you? "

" Not to my knowledge."

" Are you the Mr. Heaton who writes the stories in 'The Century'? Why did n't you tell me? "

" Why should I? It 's nothing," he returned evasively, though he was pleased at the brightening flush on her face, which was paying an eloquent tribute to his work.

" It is ever so much," she answered, so earnestly that there was a slight quiver in her voice. " I have read them, and I know; and then it is so big and beautiful to do such work, to write for the people you 've never seen, but who want to see and know you."

Her whole face was glowing with her girlish enthusiasm, and Heaton told himself that he had never before known how beautiful she could be, when she was stirred below her surface of gay society mannerism. Nevertheless, he met her words with a little laugh, although he was unable to conceal all his satisfaction at her praise, as he answered, —

" You are making too much of a small affair, Miss Tiemann. A dozen stories of no particular merit will scarcely rank me among the immortals. Moreover, I like best that my friends should forget I ever write, so I shall ask you to keep my secret while I am here."

The girl's face fell.

"And may n't I even tell Auntie?"

"I would rather not, if you don't care. A year ago, even, I should n't have minded; but the future is all so uncertain that I like to say as little as possible about my work. As a favor to me, please," he added gently.

It was not the first time since they had met that he had referred to the future in this tone of gravity. Elinor was unable to read his meaning, and something in his face made her feel that it was better not to ask.

"Well, if you won't let me tell, I suppose I must n't," she said resignedly; "only it 's not quite fair not to let us burn just a little bit of incense before you. 'T is n't every day that we get a real, live lion at Idlewilde, and we 'd like to hear him roar a little. Is this what you are writing, all the time?" she asked suddenly.

Heaton nodded.

"Yes. But how did you know?"

"Oh, gossip flies, and Napoleon's voice is louder than he thinks," she replied lightly, although she blushed as she realized the true cause of her interest in his answer. Notwithstanding the fact that the present week would

2   17

put an end to their acquaintance, she was secretly glad to discover that her companion was not engaged to some other woman. At least it gave more freedom to their temporary intercourse.

Heaton, unconscious of the interpretation which Napoleon had put upon his devotion to his pen, was unable to read the cause of her blush. In spite of his pleasure at her praise, he was sorry that she had found him out, and he determined to throw himself upon her mercy.

"You know how these people talk," he said; "and you have found out, to-day, how they martyrize the stranger within their gates. They have no perspective in such matters. If they were to hear that I'd ever written a word that was salable, they would demand an auction of stories for the benefit of the melodeon, to supplement your singing."

"But Auntie is n't like that," she urged.

" I know," he said; " only — "

He was silent for a moment, rowing steadily. Then he dropped his oars, as he said, with an evident effort, —

" The fact is, Miss Tiemann, I have n't written much lately. Till I came here, I had n't touched a pen for weeks, and I may give it up entirely."

" Oh, why? " she asked eagerly.

" Stern necessity. It's too long and too dull a story to tell, so I won't bore you with it. Still, I care enough for my writing so that it will be hard for me to let it go. I'm sorry to be so mysterious about it," he added, with a forced lightness of manner; "but now I have told you so much, I'm going to ask you to say nothing about my work, and, so far as you can, to forget it."

He bit his lip for a moment, while the water flew past them, lashed to foam under his quick strokes. Then he looked up again, and, though his lips were smiling, there was an expression in his brown eyes which somehow made her think of an animal in pain.

"If you ever do come across any of my work again," he said; "deal with it as gently as you can."

Awed by the intensity of his manner, Elinor let fall the letters, and held out her hand in token of agreement.

"I will," she said slowly.

CHAPTER THREE

"I DIMLY suspect that I made a fool of myself," Heaton remarked to himself, while he was putting his tent in order, the next day. "I hate scenes; but that girl nearly led me into making one, and now she must think me a cross between a milksop and a Don Juan. Fancying my talking melodramatically of *the future!*" He laughed, but his laugh had nothing mirthful in it. Then, when he had finished his labors, he strolled across to his hammock and threw himself down at full length, while he considered how best to remove the disagreeable impression he might have created.

Child as he thought Miss Tiemann, still he cared for her good opinion, and he disliked to have her carry away with her the idea that he was given to forcing his confidence upon comparative strangers in any such way as this. As a general thing, Heaton kept his feelings to himself. Even Jack, his constant companion, had little idea of the real inner life of his cousin, so it was all the more surprising that he had been betrayed into speaking as earnestly as he had done, the day before. At the time, he had been sincere enough; but now it seemed to him an unwarranted display of sentiment. His brown cheeks grew hot at the memory, and he had a passing desire to run down to Chicago, that day, and telegraph Jack to meet him there.

"But what is the use?" was his philosophical second thought. "I sha'n't see the girl again after this week, and she has forgotten it all by this time, most likely, so I may as well make the most of the present good times, and not care what she thinks of me. Confound those letters, though!"

For a moment he lay still and looked about him. Camp Idlewilde was at its best, that breezy July noon, for a heavy rain, the night before, had washed all heat and dust away, and every tent and every green tree and tuft of grass was fresh and smiling in the sunshine. Up in the cabin on the hill, a boy choir from the city were giving their daily hour of practice to a chorus from one of the greater oratorios. Though too far away to distinguish the words, Heaton enjoyed the rhythmic beat of their fresh young voices, and he marvelled that those clear, sweet tones could come from the restless little imps who pervaded the camp at other hours, shrieking in shrill, discordant glee. Outside the cabin, a dozen rabbits were stupidly hopping about, or stopping short to sit up and listen to the voices of their quondam enemies. On both sides of him lay the tents, scattered about among the trees, and beyond it all stretched the lake, shining like a broad, silvery mirror between its sloping banks. Napoleon and his kindred were away, and the camp was very quiet.

Five minutes later, Heaton rolled out of his hammock, gave himself the shake which, in camp, answered for his mid-day toilet, and strode away to the farm. He found Elinor swinging in her hammock under the oak-trees on the lawn. Throwing aside her book, she welcomed him cordially.

" Auntie is lying down," she said, as, without rising, she stretched out her hand to him. " Everybody here but myself takes an after-dinner nap, and I get desperately lonely, while I wait for them to wake up. Bring out that chair on the piazza and entertain me."

He obeyed her, and settled himself at her side.

" How shall I proceed? " he asked.

" Talk to me about — about yourself," she said audaciously.

" But why? There are so many more interesting subjects," he said languidly.

" What are they? "

" Thank you for the implied compliment," he returned.

"Tell me about your sister, then, if you won't talk about yourself," she responded, laughing.

"Bertha? There's not much to tell. She lives in New York, and she has two children, and I live with her."

"And her husband, I suppose. Is she as Eastern as you are?"

"How do you mean? Am I Eastern?"

"In every way. The first moment I heard you speak, I knew you came from the effete civilization of the East. All your words, your vowels, that is, sound so unlike ours. You must notice the difference. And then you don't look like the men here."

"Not even Napoleon?" he asked, as he shifted his position and sat with his elbow on the back of his chair, his head resting on his hand. He had a habit of staring intently at the ground while he was talking, and only glancing up now and then, as some especial point in the conversation awakened his interest. In some men it would have been awkward; but it seemed too characteristic of him to admit of any criticism.

"Napoleon isn't a fair type," she answered. "He is unique; but that German friend of yours is more like our Western men. I had a cousin at Harvard, a few years ago."

"Who was he, and what was his year? It's

absurd to ask, of course; but one always tries to pick up common acquaintances."

"Wilson was his name. He was in Eighty-five, I think."

"That was my year. Was Jim Wilson your cousin?"

"I feel better," Elinor declared gravely. "If you once find a common acquaintance, you are old friends directly. I've never seen Jim, to be sure; but it is a comfort to know that you have. It bridges the chasm of the unknown past."

"The most I remember about him," Heaton confessed; "is that he was called the laziest man in our class. He was a bright fellow; but he went through college such a mass of conditions that the other fellows used to say he couldn't have made even an unconditional surrender."

Elinor laughed.

"That's Jim," she said. "I recognize the fidelity of your description. But we mustn't stay here and slander my cousin. If it isn't too warm, let's walk to the spring. I'll be ready in a moment."

In an incredibly short time, she joined him, dressed for walking. Heaton cast an approving glance at her cheviot gown and little brown shoes.

"I hope you are dressed for a rough tramp,"

he said. "I want to show you one of my favorite brooks, and it looks a little as if we might get a shower."

To her surprise she had never seen him in a brighter, more careless mood. His manner, the day before, had made a profound impression on her, an impression which it had been impossible for her to shake off. After dwelling upon the matter throughout the morning, after magnifying it, according to the fashion of girlhood, it was rather a disappointment to her to find her moody, mysterious knight suddenly transformed into the genial man of the world. Still, she felt more at home with him in his present mood, and her own gayety came back to her in full measure, as they tramped away up the road at a round pace, talking blithely as they went. It was a new experience for her to find some one who loved the country as she did; and Heaton's pleasure in every woodland thing was a constant source of delight. Challenge him as she would, she could find no bird-note of which he was ignorant, no flower with which he was unfamiliar.

An hour later, they were sitting on a rugged hillside. To the right hand and the left, the branches of the trees hung low about them, caressing the tops of the green ferns that, thick and soft, waved lazily in the summer breeze. Close at their feet, a little brook went splashing over tiny waterfalls and chattering along the pebbles, on its way to a ruined waterwheel, six hundred feet below.

All at once and without preface, Elinor broke the silence which had fallen between them.

"Have you ever written anything but short stories, Mr. Heaton?"

His eyes were still fixed on the laughing, dancing water, though he roused himself at her question.

"No, that is all."

"Why don't you try a novel?" she asked.

He smiled thoughtfully.

"I am afraid it would be beyond me," he said half mischievously. "I don't believe I have had the necessary experiences."

For a minute she watched him closely. His tone was quiet and dreamy, and his face expressed full content. It was new to her that he should speak like this in regard to his writing, and she liked the mood. It was as if, soothed by the quiet beauty of the hour, he had forgotten himself and her, in his vague plans for future work.

"You must get the experience," she returned. "I think you could write a successful novel, if you were to try."

"It's not to be had for the mere asking," he answered, still in the dreamy undertone he had used before. "I have a notion that a book can't be made to order, but that it must grow up with us, if it is to amount to anything."

Elinor looked puzzled.

"I am afraid I don't quite understand."

This time he turned to look directly at her, while his face lighted with his thought.

"I don't wonder, for I did n't make it very clear. What I'm trying to get at is this: that our work is n't anything outside of ourselves. It's a part of us, and grows with our growth. That is one reason that failure tears us to pieces so. We feel that the fault is n't in our work; it's in ourselves."

"But you will write a novel in time?" she urged.

"Some day, perhaps. I have often thought of it, and wished I could do it; but it is beyond me now. If the time ever comes that I dare attempt it, I shall try."

"I hope it will come soon," she said, while she stroked the long feathery ferns at her side. "It would be so interesting to feel that perhaps this very summer had played some part in it."

She spoke with the simple egotism of a child who tries to share the mood of an older companion. Suddenly, to her surprise, she saw Heaton's lips twitch nervously, while the color faded from his face.

"What rubbish we're talking!" he said

sharply, as he hurled a stone into the pool below him and sat frowning to see the clear water grow dark with the up-turned sand.

She looked at him with startled eyes.

"What do you mean?"

"Only that my writing days are over, and I shall do nothing more. Come, Miss Tiemann, I think the shower will catch us soon, and we must be starting for home." His momentary passion appeared to have spent itself, as he stooped to offer her his hand.

She rose reluctantly.

"Must we go? This has been so pleasant, and it is almost my last chance to revel like this."

He looked down at her with his old, kindly smile.

"What do you do at other times?" he asked.

"I'm a model of decorum. When I'm at home, except when I'm practising, I sew embroidery, and make calls, and read Walter Pater. Once in a while, a very long while, I go to a party. Do you like parties?"

"What do you think?"

She eyed him narrowly.

"Ye — es," she said; "but not to distraction. Your sister and your cousin drag you into them, I think; but you like to run away and sit in a corner and look on. And yet you do know how to waltz," she added musingly; "and that is something. Most people waltz like either snakes or frogs."

"Thank you for admitting so much. But you've about hit the truth of the matter. I like society in moderate doses; but unfortunately it does n't like me."

"Why not? Anybody can be popular that wants to."

"I don't know as it's worth the trouble," he answered, a little cynically.

She looked up at him with a sudden flash of disapproval in her dark eyes.

"I don't see why you speak like that, Mr. Heaton. It is n't honest. If you did n't care about being popular, you would n't stop to think whether people like you or not."

"Perhaps you are right," he said meekly; "only one has to pay such a price for social success, nowadays, that it hardly seems worth while."

"Stop sneering at society," she commanded. "It is very good to me always, and I shall fight for it. But here comes the storm. Let's run to that cottage, down the road."

Breathless, they reached the cottage just as the rain swept down upon them. On the steps, Elinor paused and looked up at Heaton with dancing eyes.

"When you do write your great novel, Mr. Heaton, please put me into it, and be sure to state that, even if I do love society, I am admirably fitted to bear up under the hardships of country life."

"I'll put you in, just as you are," he retorted; "without any alterations or reservations, and it will be as good as making you a present of a pocket mirror."

In answer to their knock an old German woman, wrinkled like a withered apple, appeared in the doorway and led them into her neat kitchen. There she gave them chairs, then seated herself at her low spinning-wheel and fell to work again, while from time to time her little dark eyes wandered towards her stranger guests.

With a ready tact and friendliness which seemed to Heaton one of the most charming phases of her character, Elinor had answered the old woman's broken English in her own tongue. She spoke German musically and fluently rather than correctly, and Heaton's more perfect command of the language made him listen with amusement to her odd slips and errors, while they drew near to watch the humming wheel.

Shyly at first, the old woman explained to them that she bought a little wool, now and then, to spin yarn for her husband's socks. It was pleasant work for her. She loved the dear little wheel she had brought from the Fatherland, twelve years before; and, while she spun, there often came to her the thought of the far-off days in the little house at home, only — she interrupted herself complainingly, the wool was poor and broke often, not like what she had used in the old country.

"*Hier es ist Alles zu kurz, zu kurz* — Here it is all too short, too short."

Then she forgot her grumbling, as Elinor begged her to tell about her old home and friends. Won by the girl's bright, friendly manner, she talked on and on, until a sudden burst of sunshine, slanting across the floor, announced that the shower was ended.

Elinor rose.

"We must go now; but we have had a charming hour here. I am going home in a day or two; but may I come again, next summer?" she said, holding out her hand in farewell.

"*Ach, it is wie die wool,*" answered the woman quickly; "*Alles zu kurz, zu kurz; aber* come back, next summer, and bring your *freund mit.*"

"If he will be brought," returned the girl gayly. "I shall come, anyway."

As they drew near the farm, a half-hour later, Mrs. Mackie met them on the lawn.

"I am sorry to carry you off, Elinor," she said, as she held out her hand to Heaton; "but I promised to bring you over to the Inn, as soon as you came back. There is some kind of a frolic going on over there, and they want you. Mr. Heaton, we shall count on your coming over here to supper, to-morrow night. It is our last evening here, you know, so you must n't fail us."

Elinor stood looking after him, as he walked away towards the camp.

"What can be the mystery about his writing?" she said to herself half impatiently.

CHAPTER FOUR

WHEN Heaton appeared, the next afternoon, Elinor sat on the piazza, entertaining a number of friends who had unexpectedly come over from the hotel to bid her good-by. As she saw him walking across the lawn, she rose and went forward to meet him. He came towards her with a light, quick step, looking up and down among the group before him, evidently with the design of discovering her and going directly to her side. However, as she went towards him, he passed her by without a sign of recognition, halted for a moment to look again at the people before him, and then bent over her aunt's chair. A moment later, Elinor heard him asking for herself.

"Behold me!" she said at his elbow. "But is this the way you treat your hostess? I went to meet you, and you passed me by on the other side."

She was surprised at the sudden change in his face. For a moment, the color left his cheeks; then it returned and swiftly mounted to his hair. He laughed a little nervously.

3

"Forgive an absent-minded man, Miss Tiemann, even if he hasn't any manners. I was so absorbed in seeing you that I didn't see you at all."

"You have made a most wily answer, Mr. Heaton. But come, let me introduce you to my friends."

• In the gathering dusk, they were still sitting on the piazza, talking with the friendly, informal courtesy which quickly passes from more general topics to the personal details of plans and doings. Even more than her niece, Mrs. Mackie had enjoyed the young man whom chance had thrown in her way. Their daily intercourse during the past week had only increased the liking she had at once felt on meeting him, and she sincerely regretted that their parting, the next day, was to be final. It had been one of those rare cases when a chance acquaintance of a summer day had quickly ripened into a mutual regard founded upon similar tastes and common interests. Moreover, though his ease and courtesy showed him a man accustomed to the social world, there was an added charm in Heaton's manner which had attracted Mrs. Mackie far more than the young men she was in the habit of meeting. It was impossible for her to analyse it. In a weaker man, it would have been gentleness; in a less genial man, it might have been called sadness; but in his strong self-reliant manhood, it only added a flavor of mellowness, like the taste which the sun gives to the reddened side of the peach.

"I wished Mrs. Rose owned anything but a melodeon, so that Elinor could sing for us," Mrs. Mackie was saying, when she was suddenly interrupted by a noise of flying feet and rumbling wheels.

Elinor sprang to her feet.

"What is it?"

A crash answered her question; there followed a sudden outcry, and then all was still. Heaton leaped down from the piazza and rushed away across the lawn. In an instant, he was back again.

"Can you get me a lantern? There has been a runaway, and one girl is hurt. Where can I find some water?"

For the next half-hour, all was confusion. It was as if the sudden shock had broken the stillness of the summer night into countless jarring discords. Lanterns were moving to and fro, casting dull, reddish shadows over the group clustered about the wreck in the road and throwing a glare over the prostrate figure of the young girl who lay unconscious in the dust. Mrs. Mackie and Elinor were bending over her, while Heaton stood by, lantern in hand, vainly endeavoring to quiet her terrified companions.

Mrs. Rose had hurried into the house, to get

a bed in readiness, and, at the first sign of returning consciousness, the girl was lifted and carried into the farmhouse. The door closed behind the women; the men went back to pick up the ruins of their carriage, and Heaton was left alone. He threw himself down into a chair and gave a sigh of utter weariness. He felt strangely exhausted after the half-hour of excitement and the strain of helping to lift the plump young country girl. It was his first emergency case, and it had made him deathly sick to stand over her and watch her as she lay there. Jack would have been in his element; it was just in his line. Mrs. Mackie had been cool and collected, and even Elinor, girl as she was, had surprised him by her efficiency. She appeared to know by instinct just what to do and how it ought to be done; and although her voice had trembled, her hands were quite steady. He had really been the one of them all to be most unnerved; but he hoped that he had not shown it. Too bad to have his last evening spoiled in any such way, when he had been anticipating it so much!

Just then the door of the inner room opened, and Elinor came out.

"Auntie wants to know, Mr. Heaton, if you are too tired to harness old Dexter and drive me to the village. The men are all away, and we must have a doctor here as soon as possible,

and somebody ought to go for the girl's sister.
I'm sorry to trouble you; but—"

Heaton started up eagerly.

"I'm glad to do it. I was just wishing I
could be of some use, and at least I can drive
Dexter. How is she?"

"We can't tell yet how much she is hurt; but
she seems to be suffering. We have been trying
to make her as comfortable as we can, and then
Auntie sent me to find you."

"I'll go at once," he said, as he moved
towards the door.

"But why couldn't you go alone?" she asked
suddenly. "Then I could stay here and help
Auntie."

Heaton looked his disapproval. It was one
thing to go for a long drive with Miss Tiemann;
it was quite a different matter to go jogging off
by himself over country roads. He knew Dexter's customary pace, and he felt that he could
not bear it alone. He fibbed shamelessly.

"I'm not sure of the way; besides, I think a
woman ought to be the one to tell her sister."

In spite of her excitement, the dimples came
into Elinor's cheeks at his reply. Then she
said,—

"I'll go. I will be ready in a moment."

"Put on something warm," Heaton cautioned
her. "It will be cool, driving, and you mustn't
take cold."

It was a relief to Heaton to be driving along the quiet road, under the peaceful light of the stars. The stillness about him made the confusion of the past hour seem strangely unreal, like an ugly dream. Although some explanation of his present position might be a necessity, it was impossible for him to realize what had just been passing. At least, he had the certainty of Miss Tiemann's society for the next hour or two, and he felt his spirits rise at the thought.

Elinor shivered slightly.

"Are you cold?" he asked instantly, while he turned to adjust her little fur cape.

"Oh, no; I dressed warmly. How dark it is! Can you see to drive?"

"Of course. Anybody can drive this thing; it's slower than death. Did you see the girl again?"

"She's no better, and Auntie told me to hurry. She may be hurt internally, and the sooner a doctor sees her, the better."

Heaton gave a vicious cut of the whip across Dexter's chubby flanks. Dexter responded with an assenting convulsion of his hind legs, and then resumed his former meditative pace.

"Confound this beast!" Heaton said despairingly. "I believe he is in league with the undertaker."

"Let me take the whip," she answered. "I

38

can goad him, while you drive. He must hurry. Is n't it all strange?"

"Very," Heaton assented with conviction. "What do you mean is strange?"

"This. When 't is n't a week since we met, that we should be rushing — trying to rush, that is — to get a doctor for a strange woman whom fate has deposited at our door. — Poor Mrs. Rose! She will have her hands full. For her sake, I am glad we are going away, to-morrow. There's no telling how long the girl will have to stay, if she lives."

"You don't think it is as bad as that?" Heaton's sickness of the past hour came over him again.

"Auntie looked anxious when we came away. It's a case, you know, that may be anything or nothing. Poor Auntie will be worn out by it all, I'm afraid; and I had never seen anything of the kind before, so I could n't be of much use."

"I was marvelling at your coolness," Heaton answered. "I could only explain it on the ground of vast experience."

Elinor laughed nervously.

"No, indeed; only the result of a few emergency lectures. It was horrible, horrible; you've no idea of it all. Let's talk about something else. I want to forget, if I can. How long do you stay here?"

"Jack comes, to-morrow night. We may be here for a week longer; then go to the Dells, and on to the head of the lakes. It is all uncertain."

"How pleasant to travel in that way! It makes our settled plans very tame in comparison. And next winter you'll spend in New York? Sha'n't you write just a very little? I shall watch for your work."

"I can't tell; but I scarcely think so. Things don't look much like it at present."

"I wish you wouldn't give up writing," she urged. Their solitary evening drive, following the unusual excitement, had suddenly made their acquaintance take on the aspect of a ripened friendship, and she spoke to him with a greater sense of intimacy than she had known till then. "Tell me about it all."

"How do you mean?" he asked quickly. "Really, there's nothing to tell, only I may not be able to write."

"No; I didn't mean that." From his abrupt change of tone, she saw that he had mistaken her meaning and supposed that she was trying to penetrate his secret. "I meant how did you ever happen to write, in the first place."

"It was foreordained from the beginning, I suppose," he replied, as he leaned over for the whip and struck Dexter a sharp blow. "I was intended for a lawyer; but it didn't suit me half so well as writing; that's all. Now the game is played out, and I shall stop."

"And go back into law?" she asked, thinking that she read the secret of his aversion to the future in the need that he should devote himself to an uncongenial profession.

"It is doubtful. If you were a man, Miss Tiemann, you would know that there are times when we can only stand still and wait to see what will come next. I am in one of those times now. By next summer, it will probably all be settled."

"And then you will come up here and tell us all about it?" she said eagerly.

He shook his head.

"I shall have looked my last at Camp Idle-wilde, long before that time. Next year, though, I hope you will give a stray thought to our week together, Miss Tiemann. It has certainly been varied in its nature."

"Next year," she answered as frankly as a child; "Auntie and I both shall miss you, for it has been very pleasant, this acquaintance of ours. But if you are such a wanderer, you'll probably run across us again."

"My wandering days are over," he replied sadly. "Now I shall have to settle down."

It was easy to find the doctor and send him galloping out to the farm; but there was a long delay before the sister could be roused from her heavy sleep and made to understand that she must dress and go with them. The drive back to the farm was apparently much longer than the distance to the village had been. Any personal conversation between Elinor and Heaton was out of the question. The girl was trying to soothe and comfort her terrified companion, and Heaton scarcely spoke, while he allowed Dexter to shamble on at his own pace. He was listening to Miss Tiemann, admiring her kindly tact, and wishing that her clear, low voice would speak to him so sympathetically if trouble should ever come to him, as it must inevitably do.

The past week had been so short, so happy! Their pleasant friendship had been such a delight to him, for, although he might easily have been a popular man, in reality he made few friends. This might have meant much to him, if circumstances had been different. As it was, it was all beginning and no end: a few hours on the water, a walk, a drive, and all their talk which had gone to show that they might have been such good friends. The future might have been so bright before him; but he dared not look towards it now. He could only shut his eyes to it all, and stumble blindly onward.

CHAPTER FIVE

" AND how is the invalid? " Heaton asked, the next morning.

" Better," Elinor answered, as she buttoned her gloves. " At least, we infer so, for her temper is asserting itself. We heard sounds of strife, this morning, while we sat over the breakfast table, wondering whether or not she was likely to die. Moreover, she scorned the hot milk that the doctor ordered, and demanded fried eggs. I think she will recover."

" After all our lurid experience, last night, it sounds rather like an anticlimax," Mrs. Mackie observed. " Of course, I did n't want her to be injured seriously; but it would have been a little more artistic if she had remained the pensive invalid until after our departure."

" If you wished something artistic, Mrs. Mackie, you should have listened to Miss Tiemann's efforts at conversation, last night. She entirely dismissed probabilities, and adopted ' art for art's sake ' as her motto. I heard her assuring the woman that she knew just how it was, she always wanted to go to bed early, herself, after she had done a hard day's washing."

" Please don't, Mr. Heaton. I was utterly demoralized, and I had n't the least idea what I was talking about. It was n't fair for you to sit by and listen, when you ought to have helped me out."

Heaton gave her a laughing, sidelong glance.

" I licked Dexter," he said defensively. " That was enough for one man to do."

" We shall be at Crawford's for two weeks," Mrs. Mackie said. " If Miss Winnie should come to an untimely end, do telegraph us. It 's wicked to laugh, though, for the poor creature was terribly hurt, last night."

" So was I once. I tumbled down the back stairs and broke my collar-bone, when I was two years old," remarked Elinor; " but you 've laughed several times since then."

" Where do you go from Crawford's ? "

Heaton's question broke in upon one of those pauses which so frequently come when friends are waiting for the moment to say good-by. They were sitting on the piazza, surrounded by luggage, while they waited for the stage which was to take them to the station; and, according to his promise, Heaton had come over to see them off. To his surprise, he found the approaching parting harder than he had supposed it could be; and, in spite of his light, bantering conversation, his face was unusually grave as, from time to time, he glanced at Elinor, who

44

sat beside him on the uncomfortable wooden " settee."

" We shall be in and out among the mountains till October. Then we shall go home, and I shall fall to work at my music," Elinor answered, while she endeavored to tighten the roll of her umbrella. " I mean to try, this year, to see if there's any music in me. I have played with it till now; but, this last week, I have been making up my mind to work in earnest. I think I owe you the inspiration, Mr. Heaton."

" Let me." Heaton held out his hand for the umbrella. " How do you mean? " he asked, as he slowly rolled it in his slim, muscular hands.

" 'If you must, you must,' " Elinor quoted. " Have you forgotten your own theory? "

He smiled at the recollection.

" I wish you success, the success which comes in the ability to work on and on forever, with nothing to come between you and your profession."

" I'd rather rest a little, once in a while," she answered lightly; but she added to herself, " How he does hate law! "

The stage came lumbering up to the gate and stopped. In the confusion that followed, there was no opportunity for anything but the most hurried of farewells. Then the stage went on again, jolting and rumbling along in the midst of a cloud of dust. At the turn of the road, Elinor leaned out of the window and looked back. Heaton was still standing in the gateway, bending slightly forward and gazing intently after them. She waved her hand; he answered. The next instant the stage had swung around the turn, out of sight. Heaton stood there for a moment longer, looking at the empty landscape before him. Then he slowly drew his hand across his forehead while, half unconsciously, he repeated the words the old German woman had used, the day before, —

"*Es ist Alles zu kurz, zu kurz.*"

Crossing the lawn on his way back to the camp, he passed near the hammock. There on the ground lay a little book which Elinor had dropped, the afternoon before, and, in the evening's excitement, she had forgotten it. Heaton stooped and took it up. It was only a summer novel, rather shabby, with her name written across the cover, and a leaf turned down to mark the place where she had stopped reading. The young man held it irresolutely for a moment; then, with a hasty glance at the house, he tucked it into the side pocket of his short gray coat and walked away, whistling softly to himself.

Heaton was unusually late in going down to the log cabin, at dinner time. Nearly all the campers had left the tables when he appeared, and he showed little disposition to enter into conversation with those that were left. Afterwards, without going for his customary row, he went directly to his hammock, where he spent the greater part of the afternoon lying on his back with his hands clasped under his head, and staring up into the green trees above him. Hour by hour, the last week passed in review before his eyes; but he dwelt longest on three pictures which stood out clearly from the rest: Elinor in a pink gown against a pinker sunset sky; Elinor staring at him with an eager, flushed face, and dropping the letters into her lap while she stretched out her hand to bind herself to her agreement; and Elinor, her hair all ruffled by the storm and her face full of merriment, bending down beside the old German woman to watch the busy wheel.

Without stirring otherwise, he put his hand into his pocket, pulled out the little book, and began scribbling on the flyleaf.

"None of that, old man! You know that is forbidden."

He started up abruptly, cramming the book into his pocket.

"Jack? How did you get over so early?"

"Had a fit of remorse for leaving you so long, so I took an earlier train than I said I should. It's as well I did, though, for I found you in mischief. Give an account of yourself."

"I'm all right. Had a good time?"

"Don't I look so? You missed it; girls and hops innumerable, and none too many men, men like you and me, that is."

He was certainly an attractive specimen of humanity, as he sat there on the ground beside the hammock, laughing at the modesty of his own assertion. For the past twenty-three years, life had dealt kindly with Jack Wyckoff, and he showed his appreciation of its favors by growing into a handsome, hearty manhood. His blond face and strong figure roused the admiration of every woman he met; every man of his acquaintance liked him for his genial, sunny temper; but Jack went on his own way, unspoiled alike by admiration from women and popularity among men, only intent upon having a good time as he went along, and ultimately making a record in his chosen profession.

"What's been going on here?" he asked. "Is Napoleon still on deck at the campfire, and has Kurzenbeine gone back to Chicago? It looks quiet as the grave here."

"What made you hurry back?" inquired Heaton, as he rose and stretched himself.

"Devotion to you, Tom, coupled with the fact that the prettiest girl I met up there was coming down on this train. Now I look at you, though, you seem a little off. What the deuce sent you to writing again? I hope you've not done much of it." And Jack's face lost something of its jollity.

"No; only a little, but I might as well." Heaton dropped down into the hammock again, and sat scowling at the ground. " I might as well keep at it as long as I can, Jack. I'll have to give it up soon enough, anyway."

"I know, old fellow; but there's no use in expediting matters. You can't hinder the inevitable; but you may help it on a good deal. I'd let the writing alone, this summer."

There was a prolonged silence. Jack was the first to break it.

"I say, Tom, what's up? You're not the same fellow I left."

"Nothing is up. I've been playing with fire, that's all."

Jack whistled softly to himself.

"That's a highly original remark, and it usually portendeth a girl. Well?"

"Well, it was that Miss Tiemann from the farm. You know we had asked who she was before you went away. Napoleon did the deed. He introduced me to the aunt, the aunt introduced me to the niece, the niece was an uncommonly nice girl, and I behaved as you do, as I'd have done, a year ago."

"The best thing you could possibly have done. Now take me over and introduce me."

"They went, to-day."

" Oh, and you were pondering upon past joys, when I found you. I thought you looked pensive. What's the use of taking it to heart, Tom? The summer girl is omnipresent, and we'll move on in search of fresh fields. I've been through dozens of just such experiences; but they don't prey on me a little bit. We'll start for the Dells to-morrow, if you say so."

Heaton made no answer. His cousin sat looking up at him intently; and, in spite of the laugh on his lips, his merry blue eyes wore an anxious expression. Neither of them spoke, and the stillness was broken only by the ecstatic cheering of the choir boys, who were playing ball in a neighboring field. Then Heaton asked abruptly, —

" For God's sake, Jack, how long is this thing to go on?"

"On my honor, Tom, I've no idea."

"On your honor? Tell me, if you can; it's better to know."

. "I can't tell at all. I would, if I could, old man. He said it might be a month or two, it might be two or three years."

Heaton's head dropped on his hands.

" I could stand all the rest well enough; it's only the waiting and the uncertainty that are so bad. Nothing seems of any use, now, for it may not be finished."

Wyckoff rose. He had seen his cousin in

this mood before, and experience had taught him that its surest cure was to be found in physical exercise.

"I must row up to the village to send a letter," he said, as he rested his hand on his cousin's shoulder. "I wish you'd come with me, Tom. I've things to tell you, you know. Everybody made a grand row because you did n't go up, too. They wanted to wire you; but I told them you were turning hermit, and it would n't do any good. Come along. Where did you leave the boat?"

Half-way across the lake, Heaton rested on his oars.

"You're a good sort of fellow, Jack," he said slowly; "and I appreciate it, even if I don't say much about it. But, after all, if I were a murderer going to be hanged, though theoretically I suppose I should cling to every last day of my life, I've a general notion that I should bribe the Lord High Executioner to hurry up and get it over with."

CHAPTER SIX

" GIVE me your blessing, Auntie, before I go."

Mrs. Mackie looked up at the girlish figure standing before her in the doorway.

" Don't you really think I'd better go with you? " she asked.

" No; I must begin to fight my own battles at once. Besides, I shall do better if I am alone. I can't say that I anticipate it, though. Remember, you are to meet me down town, at one, so we can have lunch together before you go to the train."

She crossed the room and stood for a moment before the mirror, as if to assure herself that her dress was in perfect order. Then, without speaking, she kissed her aunt and swiftly left the room.

Once out in the street, she walked rapidly to the nearest elevated station. It was one of the clear, bright days of late September when the up-town streets of New York, though empty, yet begin to take on the look of returning life. People were still lingering at the mountains or by the sea; but their houses were being opened and aired, in preparation for their coming. Through the wide-open windows, Elinor could see the white-capped maids flying about; but the sidewalks were still deserted, save by the flock of sparrows which, without troubling themselves to move out of her way, eyed her with the calm assurance that city life brings to its every inhabitant, bird as well as human.

Half a dozen times on her way down town, Elinor looked at her watch to make sure that she would be in season for her appointment; yet, when the hour struck, she was still irresolutely pacing one of the streets in the neighborhood of Madison Square.

" Alas, my time has come ! " she said to herself. " All I can do now is to screw my courage to the sticking-place. But I won't fail. Winterbaum advised me to try, and I 'm determined to succeed. Sooner or later I will sing."

There was a bright scarlet spot in the middle of each cheek, and she shut her teeth hard upon her lower lip to steady it. Then she turned into one of the tall buildings, and, too nervous to think of the elevator, she hurried up four or five flights of stairs and paused, breathless, before a door which bore in staring black letters the sign:

MANUEL ARTURO

ENTER WITHOUT KNOCKING

Fearful lest, if she delayed, her courage would forsake her, Elinor turned the knob and entered the room. It was an attractive little place, as befitted the outer sanctum of one of America's greatest musicians; but, as Elinor sank into the nearest chair, her fear came back to her, for the sounds which met her ears were not reassuring. Directly opposite the corner where she sat, was a doorway which evidently led into the inner room where Signor Arturo was giving a lesson. The door was slightly open, and she could hear two voices, one a clear tenor which sang a few notes, only to be interrupted by an inarticulate roar from the other, followed by a vigorous pounding upon one single note of the piano.

"Up, I have told you! Up! *Up!* Put out your tongue! Carry the tone upward in the mouth!"

The tenor voice came again, wonderfully sweet and true it seemed to Elinor, as she listened.

"No, that is not right at all. Why you scream there?"

"But, Signor Arturo — " interposed the laughing voice of the pupil, who did not appear in the least discomposed by the obvious bad temper of his master.

"It is no *but;* you must do it. I have told you forty thousand times, and I tell you again, you must keep the tones up. Now sing!"

The other voice took up the phrase which she had caught, as she entered the room. There came a crash, as if two hands had suddenly descended upon all the keys within their reach.

"Up! Up! Up! Up! Again! You will never be right to sing it as you do; no? Listen to me." And he sang the same strain three or four times over, with a delicacy of shading which transformed the simple phrase into a masterpiece of art.

The tenor tried to imitate him, caught the first few notes, then stumbled, faltered, and stopped singing.

"Oh, I say, Signor Arturo, I can't do that," he said, with a jovial laugh.

"But you must. Now try. I pray you not to dismay. I never dismay."

The tenor voice came again, better, this time; but, half through the phrase, Arturo interrupted it.

"That will not do. You sing with an expression as if I were pinching you to sing, you know, and you were angry about it. All your tones are quite wrong. Next time, we shall begin with that little study."

"But how about the song?"

"You shall have no more songs until you have sung better. Now you must go; your hour is five minutes over."

Elinor caught her breath quickly, as she heard

steps coming towards the door. She looked up to see two merry blue eyes staring at her, as the younger man passed out through the room. Then she looked down again, for Signor Arturo stood before her.

"You wish me?" he asked, in a more genial tone which partially reassured her.

"I am Miss Tiemann. I wrote to make an appointment with you," she answered, forcing herself to meet his eyes.

She saw nothing more formidable than a stout, dark little man who stood staring at her and polishing his bald head with his handkerchief. She was conscious of a momentary wonder how so small a body could contain so great a voice; then she listened in dismay to his next words.

"You were sent by Winterbaum, my old pupil, I think; and you wish to make an appointment for me to try your voice."

"Can't you do it now?" she said blankly.

"Certainly not. My time is full, each day; and the next pupil will be here at once. Give me your address, please." And he took a little memorandum book from his pocket.

"Oh, I can't wait," she exclaimed. "I must know, to-day."

His face grew grim. He was not accustomed to having his pupils assert themselves in this fashion.

"Not if it is a question of studying with me.

Winterbaum should have told you that. I can give you the time on Thursday, the tenth."

"Not till then? That is two weeks off."

He shook his head and tapped his book impatiently.

"It must be that, or nothing."

"I 'll take it, then; but I hoped —"

"What is your voice?"

"Soprano."

"And the course of study you wish to take?"

"Herr Winterbaum said he thought I was best fitted for oratorio," she faltered.

"And your address?"

She gave it; then, too much astonished to rebel, she obeyed his gesture of dismissal.

Outside the door, she stopped short and stared at the panels for a moment.

"Oh, the little monster!" she said slowly.

From the end of the hallway, she heard a low, irrepressible laugh. Turning suddenly, she saw the young man who had left the room just ahead of her, standing by the door of the elevator shaft.

"Please excuse me," he said quickly, as he took off his hat. "I ought n't to have laughed; but I really could n't help hearing, and I agreed with you perfectly. Did you have a bad time?"

"Dreadful."

Their eyes met, and they laughed again.

"I know all about it; I 've just been there.

But you must have had the benefit of part of my lesson."

" Is he often like this?" Elinor's tone betrayed her indignation.

"No; not often. He 's unusually tempestuous, to-day. Then you don't study with him?"

"Not yet; but I hope I am going to. He has n't tried my voice yet."

" I hope you will succeed. It is n't every one who does, I can tell you. I had to wait for more than two years before he would even look at me. Here comes the elevator, at last." And he stood aside to let Elinor pass in before him. " I wish you all manner of success," he said, as they parted at the street door. " It is n't always an unmitigated delight to be a pupil of Arturo; but, after all, you will never regret your choice of teacher." And bowing again, he turned away and left her.

" Is n't it discouraging?" Elinor said over her bouillon, an hour later.

" I feel as if I did n't know what to do," said Mrs. Mackie anxiously. "Your uncle is to meet me in Cleveland, to-morrow, or I should n't think of leaving you. As it is—"

" As it is, you will go," interrupted Elinor. " There is no use in your waiting here with me. If I succeed, all my arrangements are made for staying; if I fail, I can pack my trunk and take the first train that leaves for the West. In either

case, you couldn't help me. Of course, I'd
rather have had the matter settled, to-day, when
I was nerved up to the crisis, and before my new
gown had lost its pristine freshness. Still, I don't
think he's a man to be unduly influenced by such
little matters as imported gowns."

"But what will you do in the mean time?" her
aunt asked doubtfully. "Till your lessons begin,
I mean."

"Kill time as fast as I can, Auntie. It won't
be pleasant; but I can endure it, and there's no
sense in your staying here, when you know
you hate New York. It seems years to me,
though, since that last recital at home, when
Winterbaum urged me to come on here to take
lessons."

The waiter drew near, just then, and Elinor
lost herself in study of the card. When her
order was given, she looked up with a little
laugh.

"Art is long; isn't it, Auntie? The only question is whether I have length of days to match
it. It seemed to me that if once I could get
started, I could work, work, work forever, for
the sake of one little taste of success at the end;
and now it is so provoking to be met at the start
with this delay. Do you think there's any
chance?"

Mrs. Mackie smiled at the impetuous question.
She glanced up at the eager face before her and

reflected how pretty her niece had grown, during the past two or three years.

" The advice of a teacher like Mr. Winterbaum ought to count for something," she replied. " I don't worry at all about your work, Elinor; but it seems to me that you are going to be rather lonely, in this new venture of yours. Your uncle and I can't very well come here to live. I wish you could have gone on studying at home for a year longer, at least."

" If I am ever to change, this is the time," she said bravely. " You need n't worry about me. As soon as I get to work, I shall be all right."

" But you can't live without friends, no matter how much you may bury yourself in your work. I do hope Allie Amidon will remember to write to her cousin about you. If she calls and is nice to you, that may be better than nothing."

Elinor pushed aside her plate.

" Poor dear little Auntie! You are determined that I shall have a very bad time of it. You forget that I'm willing to give up some other things for the sake of my voice. If I can't sing, and Arturo says so, I promise to come directly home and spend the rest of my days there."

" Yes; but," and Mrs. Mackie gave utterance to the thought which had been slowly growing up in her mind during the week that she had spent in settling her niece in the New York boarding-house; "the fact is, you are entirely too young and too pretty to be left alone in a city like this."

The girl laughed outright.

" I 'm much obliged for the compliment, and I wish you did n't grudge it so. But I 'm only a working girl here, working on my voice instead of plain sewing. I shall be quite safe. However, if danger threatens, I will promise to flee to Allie's Mrs. Emerson, without even waiting for an introduction."

She turned to pick up her gloves and, as she did so, she glanced into one of the mirrors which lined the wall. Her face brightened, as she bent forward across the table.

"Auntie," she said in a low voice; "is n't it odd? Do you remember that Mr. Heaton we met at Idlewilde, two years ago? He 's here."

" Where ? "

" Don't look. He is staring straight at us. He is right behind me, at the table in the left-hand corner, there with that yellow-headed boy. I did n't see him come in; but he must have seen us. I wonder why he did n't come over to speak to us."

As she rose to leave the table, Mrs. Mackie turned to look in the direction which Elinor had pointed out. There at the corner table sat Heaton, leaning back in his chair as if waiting to be served, and listening to the animated talk of his boy companion. There was no doubt of his being their old acquaintance; yet, even in her swift glance, Mrs. Mackie was conscious that he was much altered. He was older and thinner and graver than he had been, and his brown hair was slightly streaked with gray. Still, it was Heaton who sat before them, and she felt a keen sense of pleasure as she moved towards him, waiting to catch some look of recognition.

In going out of the room, it was necessary to pass close to the table where he was sitting. Elinor, who led the way, was watching him expectantly, ready to greet her old friend, if he looked towards them. He did look up, just as they were beside him; and both women bowed in the cordial, friendly manner which was a natural result of their acquaintance, two years before. The next moment, Elinor turned white, and, raising her head haughtily, she swept on out of the room. Their old friend had looked her full in the face; then he had turned his eyes away again indifferently, without giving any sign that he had ever seen her before.

CHAPTER SEVEN

" MISS TIEMANN?" said a voice at her door.

" Yes."

" There's some one to see you, down-stairs. She is waiting in the little parlor."

Elinor crossed the room and took the card which the maid was holding out to her on the tray.

"Mrs. Edwin Emerson," she read. "That is Allie Amidon's cousin. Tell her I'll be down directly," she added to the maid.

She was undeniably pleased at the thought of meeting her caller, for the two weeks since her aunt had gone away had been long and lonely ones to the young girl. It was one thing to come to New York to throw herself heart and soul into her chosen work; it was quite another matter to spend long, idle hours alone in her room, impatiently waiting for her work to begin, uncertain even whether it could begin at all. She could not read all the time, and she had never been an enthusiastic needlewoman; neither did she care to spend all of her hours out of doors. Exploring a city in which she saw no familiar face had palled upon her by this time, and she

63

had begun to long for congenial companionship. She went through it bravely; but this first experience of homesickness had cost her many bitter tears. However, they were shed in the privacy of her room and in the darkness of the night. By day, as she went about among the people in the boarding-house, she still maintained the gay, resolute manner she had always worn.

Since the day that her aunt had left her, she had never seen Heaton. In fact, she had little desire to meet him again. He had refused in the most direct and unequivocal manner to recognize the fact of their former acquaintance, although there could have been no doubt whatever of his having known either herself or her aunt. Ponder upon the subject as she would, Elinor could see no reason for this unexpected slight. At Idlewilde, he had not only shown himself friendly; day by day he had sought her society with eagerness, and he had parted from her with evident regret. During the days which followed their unexpected meeting, Elinor went over all the details of their acquaintance; but she could find no clue to the mystery. For one moment, she had wondered whether Heaton were the gentleman he had seemed. Then she scornfully dismissed the suspicion. It was impossible to doubt his honor, however much one might doubt his manners.

"It's simply because he thinks I am a raw Westerner, and he does n't care to know me, here in New York," she said to herself, one day, while she stood before her mirror. Then she made a scornful grimace at the face looking back at her, and resolved to content herself with that explanation and dismiss the matter from her mind.

Nevertheless, as he was the only person in the city whom she had ever seen before, it was impossible for her to forget his existence, and she found herself giving much more thought to her former acquaintance than she cared to do. She wondered whether he were finding the law as uncongenial a profession as he had seemed to expect. She wondered whether he had entirely foresworn his writing. She even wondered if he were still as intimate with Jack, that much-talked-of cousin whom she had never seen, of whose other name, even, she was ignorant. She half wished that she might meet him, some day. Perhaps he might explain to her his cousin's unwillingness to acknowledge her as an acquaintance.

She made a hasty toilet and went running down-stairs to meet her guest. In this city of strangers, the fact that Mrs. Emerson was a cousin of her own cousin, Allie Amidon, made her seem like a close relative; and Elinor felt that her anticipations were realized when she saw

5 65

the attractive little woman who rose to meet her. In the stir of greeting, of rapid interchange of question and answer which followed their coming together, there was no opportunity for Elinor to analyze her impressions. Afterwards, when she was alone in her room once more, she realized that she had been spending an hour in the society of a thorough woman of the world, a woman whose position was so assured that she could dismiss the consideration of it from her thoughts and devote herself to her domestic affairs, secure in the knowledge that her place in society was awaiting her, whenever she might choose to assume it.

Without being in the least degree handsome, Mrs. Emerson seemed to Elinor one of the most beautiful women she had ever met. Moreover, she was blest with that gift, so rare among American women, a low, musical voice, and her manners were indescribably winning. But this lay upon the surface and was seen at a glance. Beyond and beneath it, there was an innate womanliness, a quick sympathy with every one with whom she came in contact. It was this which had won for Bertha Emerson a popularity which was entirely independent of the fact that she was mistress of a beautiful home, and one of the best hostesses in all the society-loving city.

" So you see that I am Allie's own cousin, and almost related to you, even if we never have met," Mrs. Emerson said at length, as they were sitting together in the stiff little parlor. "Now tell me all about yourself. You are here to study music, I think."

Elinor laughed a little.

"I had hoped so; but there appears to be some question about it. I came on, intending to study with Arturo."

"Arturo? My cousin, Mr. Wyckoff, has been studying with him for a year, and he thinks he is wonderful. How do you like him?"

"I fear I'm not in a mood to answer that question fairly, Mrs. Emerson. I had a very bad time with him, to-day."

"My cousin says that he rages at times. I trust you did n't find him in one of his savage moods."

Elinor shook her head.

"If I did n't, I shudder to think what his savage moods may be."

Mrs. Emerson bent over and laid her hand on that of her hostess.

"Tell me all about it, dear. I know it was something uncomfortable, for you look worried, and he has the reputation of being a bear."

Elinor bit her lower lip for a moment. It was so good to be spoken to in this sympathetic tone, after living alone for two long weeks.

"It's nothing," she said bravely. "I've no right to trouble you with my worries. Besides, it was all funny, very funny, only I was feeling blue, and I could n't see it in a proper light. Have you ever seen Arturo?"

"Never. From what I know, I think I don't care to meet him."

"He is a tiny little man, very bald, and with a voice like Niagara. He talks a mixture of all the languages known at Babel."

"It's the same man," Mrs. Emerson interposed. "I recognize my cousin's description of him."

"I had an appointment with him, this morning, to have him try my voice," Elinor continued, laughing in spite of herself at the recollection. "My watch was fast, and, for five or ten minutes, I had the pleasure of hearing him scold the pupil before me. That did n't tend to put me at my ease, and when my turn did come, I could n't sing at all. My voice was perfectly unmanageable. He kept scowling more and more darkly, till at last he brought both fists down on the keys with a crash, and turned around to face me. 'You are not good, signorina,' he said. 'I cannot make a voice out of nothing. You would better buy a music box to play with.'"

"Oh, you poor child!" And Mrs. Emerson laughed.

"That was nothing to what followed. He told me that I had no voice and no ear, that nothing could tempt him to teach me. He advised me to study the piano, or harmony, or even the banjo; but I politely assured him that I only cared to sing, that I fully intended to learn, and that I preferred to have him for my teacher. Then he lost his temper, and I suspect that he swore at me a little. Unfortunately I don't understand Italian, so it was quite thrown away. Then we began again at the very beginning and argued it all out, inch by inch, neither of us yielding in the least."

Mrs. Emerson laughed again in mingled horror and amusement.

"If only I could have seen you! It must have been something new for Arturo to have anybody defy his will, for his word is law in the musical world."

"He ought to be grateful to me, then, for giving him the new experience. But it was an important matter to me. I felt as if I couldn't give up and go back home, when all my arrangements were made to stay here."

"It would have been ignominious. But go on. I must hear the rest."

"The rest was a fitting climax. After we had talked for nearly half an hour, he struck another discordant chord and said sulkily, 'I have told you that it is not of the least of use, for you never can be taught to sing. However, you may try again, if you wish to be quite sure; but it will do you no good!'"

"Encouraging!"

"Was n't it? But my temper had come, and I was too angry to be afraid of him, so I did a little better. But even that did n't suit him. He jerked himself around and said viciously, "*Diavolo*, signorina, if you can do that now, why did n't you say so in the first moment and not waste all my time, which is very costly? You are not good for anything now, for Winterbaum has taught you quite wrong; but come to me in a week from to-day, and I will see what I can do. Now go.' And I went. Do you wonder that I did n't know whether to laugh or to cry, nor which of us had come off conqueror?"

"You have, I know. But I wish I had heard the interview. Do you mind if I tell my cousin? He will be so amused."

"You may tell any one you choose," Elinor answered, laughing. "This has made me absolutely brazen, and I glory in my combativeness."

"I shall be eager to know the result of your next contest," Mrs. Emerson said, as she rose to take leave; "so you must come to see me soon and tell me about it. Tuesday is my day; but I wish you would feel free to drop in upon me at any time. I am at home a great deal. Both Mr. Emerson and my brother are home-abiding people, and we have a cat-like affection for our own chimney corner."

"You have no children?" Elinor asked.

70

"Yes, two, Ned and baby Ruth, the family tyrant. But come to see me, and I will introduce you to my great boy and my small girl. You know we are cousins, through Allie, and I shall expect you to behave in true cousinly fashion."

Elinor stood at the window, looking after her guest, as she went down the steps. All at once, her horizon seemed to have grown brighter, and New York appeared to her a much more attractive place than it had done, an hour before. And yet even she had no foreshadowing of the important part which the Emerson household was destined to play in her life.

CHAPTER EIGHT

A FEW weeks later, as Elinor dressed for her first dinner party of the season, she was quite ready to deny that she had ever been homesick. Her work had at last begun in earnest, and each day was busier and happier than the one before it had been. The second test of her voice had proved more satisfactory, and Arturo, as if moved to admiration of this tempestuous young woman, the first of all his pupils who had dared to assert herself in opposition to his opinions, had not only consented to give her two lessons a week, but was treating her with a certain courtesy which her dauntless courage would naturally arouse.

She had not seen Mrs. Emerson since the day of their first meeting. They had exchanged two or three calls in the mean time, without finding each other at home; and Elinor had begun to fear that their acquaintance was doomed to die a natural death, when she received a cordial, informal note, asking her to dinner, "not a ceremonious affair, just ourselves and half a dozen friends," ran the invitation; "so we shall expect you to be quite informal."

However, informality in New York and informality at Idlewilde, for instance, were quite different matters, Elinor reflected; and she chose her most becoming gown for the occasion. She was glad that she had done so, for, when she entered Mrs. Emerson's pleasant drawing-room, the other guests were assembled and were clothed in the conventional purple and fine linen of the day.

Mrs. Emerson greeted her with the same cordiality she had shown before, and introduced her husband, a jovial, prosperous lawyer. Then she brought up a much-bestarched little man who had been assigned to Elinor as a table companion. As they stepped slightly to one side, and entered into the aimless conversation which precedes dinner, Elinor glanced up and down the room at the people to whom she had just been introduced. There was nothing especially striking about them, and her eyes wandered over them indifferently enough, till all at once she started slightly and the color came into her cheeks.

"Who is that?" she asked, interrupting her companion in the midst of a dissertation upon the approaching horse show.

"Which?" he inquired, turning his head as far as the painful proportions of his collar would allow him to do.

"That tall, dark man who just came in. He

looks like somebody I used to know," she said carelessly.

"That? That's Tom Heaton. Don't you know him?"

"Tom Heaton?" she echoed.

"Yes, he's Mrs. Emerson's brother, and lives with her. You've probably met him here before. He used to be something of a lion, a year or so ago."

"How do you mean?" she asked, while her thoughts were busy with the man to whom she had so promptly turned her back. Strange that he should be the brother of her hostess! How tiny the world was! The situation was not exactly agreeable. Here in his sister's house, he would be forced to recognize her existence, although he had shown quite plainly, only a few weeks before, that he had no wish to keep up the acquaintance.

"Oh, he was a genius, you know, a fellow who wrote things that people raved over. I never could see much in them, myself; but I always liked Tom, he was such a good fellow, and I was awfully sorry for him, when he went blind, last winter."

Elinor caught her breath sharply and clutched the chair before her for support. The room seemed to be whirling about her, and the voice of her companion sounded remote and hollow. Heaton blind! She could not believe it. He had come walking into the room and paused to speak to his sister, with nothing in his manner to distinguish him from the other guests. There must be some mistake. It could not be the same Heaton with whom she had walked and rowed at Idlewilde.

Suddenly it came over her that this, beyond a doubt, was the explanation of everything which had puzzled her before. This was the reason that he must give up his writing; this was the secret of his frequent bitter reference to the future. And finally, this was the cause of his apparent slight of her, six weeks before. He had not spoken to her, for the simple reason that he had not been able to see her, though she had passed so near him that she could have touched him on the shoulder as he sat there. This, too, explained countless peculiarities of his manner, oddities which had been unnoticed at the time, but which came back to her now, in the light of this sudden revelation. Mr. Heaton, strong, active, and in the prime of his manhood, delighting in out-of-door life and all that pertained to it, to be stricken with blindness and shut out from all that he so enjoyed! She rallied with an effort. The brain works swiftly at such times, and when she regained her self-control, her companion was still dwelling upon the same topic. She was glad of that; it saved her asking any question.

"'Twas hard luck, you know. For a year or so, he had been having the world at his feet, for he was always a great man in society, and then his writing helped him on. It was sudden, too, and took us all by surprise; but they say he had known it was coming."

"What was the cause of it?" she asked, turning towards her old friend slowly, as if she dreaded the moment when she must look him in the face.

"Some kind of a strain, I don't know just what. I was abroad all that year, and he and Wyckoff went off together somewhere, just after the trouble developed, so I never knew exactly how it was. Did you say you knew him?"

"I met him a few times, two or three years ago; but I had heard nothing about him since, nor about — this."

As she spoke, she raised her eyes and looked at him. He was standing directly opposite her, talking with the same boy whom she had seen lunching with him. One or two men stood near him, taking an occasional part in the conversation; and, as his face became animated, something in his expression reminded her of the day in the cottage, when he had laughed at her German. It was the same genial, kindly smile she had known; but it vanished more quickly, and at rest his face was very sad.

"That's Ned Emerson with him," her companion explained. "They are great friends, and Heaton is as proud of the boy as if he were his own son. If you like, I'll bring him over to you — after dinner, that is," he added, as there came a general move towards the dining-room.

A glance over her shoulder had told Elinor that Heaton and the boy were the last ones to leave the drawing-room. As she settled herself in her place at the table, she bent over to catch the remark of her talkative little neighbor; and, in doing so, she discovered that Heaton was seated at her other hand. For a moment, she was silent, not knowing how to address him, not daring to speak to her other neighbor, for fear that Heaton might recognize her voice. He must know she was there, she reflected, and she wished that he would take the initiative. It was impossible for her to talk to him as she would have done to the Heaton she used to know. This was to all intents and purposes another man. She felt a sudden awe creeping over her, as she stole an appealing glance up at him, in the vain hope that he would speak. But Heaton remained obstinately silent, with an odd little smile on his lips, half bored, half amused. It was the first time she had seen him in evening dress. She studied the careless ease with which he wore it, and she made a mental comparison which was not entirely flattering to her little companion, who was chattering volubly in a futile attempt to hold her wandering attention. All at once, he wound up with, —

"But what do you think about it, Miss Tiemann?"

Elinor started and blushed guiltily.

"I'm — I'm sure I don't know what to think," she faltered. Then abruptly she turned to Heaton. "Mr. Heaton, I wonder if you have forgotten Idlewilde?" she asked, in a voice which seemed to her to proceed from the roof of her mouth.

Instantly his face changed.

"It really is the same Miss Tiemann? Bertha spoke of you often, and I have wondered if it could be my old acquaintance."

"The very one," she said. "Fate has cast me at your door, just as it cast Miss Winnie at our door, two years ago. Do you remember that night?"

"Do you think I could ever forget my struggles with Dexter?" he answered, with a smile. "No; my memory is a good one, and I think I could give you a fairly accurate history of that week. How long have you been in New York?"

He was obliged to wait for his reply, for Elinor's other neighbor was claiming his share of attention, and she had turned back to him. Now that the ice was broken, she would gladly have given her time entirely to Heaton; but, as the conversation became more general, it was impossible for them to exchange more than an occasional word or two. She watched him closely, however, and, as her eyes rested on his face, she was always conscious of that same feeling of mingled awe and pity, the same desire to avoid his sightless stare. He was glad to meet her again, it was evident; but she could read his embarrassment by countless signs which told her he was ill at ease and trying to conceal it all underneath that brave little smile. As she left the table, she turned to him.

"Come and talk to me as soon as you are at liberty," she said in a low voice. "I am longing to gossip with you about Idlewilde."

Before the other men had left the table, Heaton excused himself and went back to the drawing-room. Mrs. Emerson was sitting with Elinor, a little at one side of the room; and, as her brother came slowly towards them, she called him to her.

"Miss Tiemann has been telling me that you are old friends, Tom," she said, as she rose; "and you must have ever so much to talk over. Take my place, and excuse me for a while. I must go and speak to Mrs. Bennett."

There was a long pause after she went away. Heaton had stretched out his hand to feel for the back of the chair, and then, seating himself, he had turned towards Elinor. Something in the gesture sent a chill through her. It seemed to intensify the impression made by the brown eyes which met hers so squarely and so unconsciously; and yet it was impossible for her to realize that he could not see her, as she sat there in her pretty evening gown, playing nervously with one long-stemmed pink rose. If he would only turn his eyes away, it would not be so bad. Perhaps then she could think of something to say. She looked helplessly up and down the room in search of some subject of conversation. The pause grew more and more strained, and she felt that she must break it.

"What an early winter we are having," she said at length.

Heaton smiled a little tired, sad smile. He had never been slow to read people; and, during the past year, as if to balance his loss of sight, his other senses had become more acute. He could fancy just how she was sitting there, blushing and frowning a little in her effort to appear at ease; but, oddly enough, in the picture which came before him, she was sitting in the stern of a boat, and the lap of her blue cheviot gown was strewn with unopened letters.

"Yes," he assented quietly; "and if you are n't used to them, you will find our east winds very trying. How long since you came?"

"Only six weeks," she answered, giving an impatient gesture which snapped off the stem of the heavy rose in her hand. "It seems longer, for it was so long before I went to work."

"You have been successful since I saw you," he went on, as if anxious to avoid another pause.

He was still sitting with his face turned towards her, and to avoid his eyes Elinor kept her own eyes obstinately fixed on the floor. In a way, it helped on the illusion that she was talking to the man she had formerly known. His voice was the same; she recalled all its little intonations and turns of expression, its peculiar low distinctness.

"That depends on what you call success," she answered, with an effort at lightness. "All I have done yet is to prove my right to go on; it remains to be seen how far I go."

"Were you at Idlewilde, last year?"

"Of course, and this summer, too. The old place is unchanged."

"Even Napoleon?" he asked, while his face lighted with a sudden flash of fun.

"I see that you have a good memory," she replied, conscious that her words had a flat, conventional sound, yet unable to speak in her usual tone. "Yes, Napoleon was there, in a brand-new suit, and your German friend came up for a week. I saw him once or twice, and he was still mourning for you. Likewise I saw Miss Winnie."

"Then she recovered?"

"She certainly did. But tell me, how long did you stay after we left?"

"Only three days," he answered. "Life was very uneventful after your departure. We experienced neither hops nor runaways, and even Napoleon palled upon us in time."

"Oh, I say, Heaton," remarked Elinor's companion at dinner, as he strolled up to them; "where's Wyckoff, these days? I have n't seen him anywhere for weeks, and I thought surely he'd be here, to-night."

Before Heaton could answer, Mr. Emerson had swept down upon Elinor and carried her off to look at his Japanese bronzes. She did not see Heaton again until just as she was taking leave of her hostess. He stood at the farther end of the room, listless and alone. Elinor looked towards him and hesitated. Then she crossed the room to his side.

"Good night, Mr. Heaton. It has been good to see you again," she said, with something of her old cordial manner.

He held out his hand.

"Good night," he answered. "I was just wondering if you had gone. Edwin carried you off too soon. May I call on you sometime with my sister?"

" Do, please. I 've dozens of things to talk over with you. I 'm nearly always in, on Tuesdays and Fridays; but I shall feel as if I ought to receive you out of doors, for the sake of tradition."

CHAPTER NINE

IT was late, that night, when Elinor fell asleep. When she reached her room, she dropped into the nearest chair, and sat there motionless for a long hour. She felt that her much-anticipated evening had been a dismal failure, and her short conversation with Heaton had been the worst part of it all. Instead of meeting him frankly upon the old ground, regardless of any change in him, she had been stiff and constrained and awkward, until he, too, had been uncomfortable and embarrassed.

Under ordinary circumstances, she would have been glad to see him again, for that far-off week at Idlewilde had always remained a pleasant memory; but now she wished that their pathways had never crossed. After once seeing him, that night, so altered and so shut out from the pretty, gay world around him, it had been impossible for her to forget that he was in the room. She had been restless and absent-minded when she was not with him; but as soon as they were left alone together, she had felt a childish desire to run away and leave him to himself once more. It was provoking, she reflected petulantly, to find him in the home of her new friends, where she could not fail to see him often. Mrs. Emerson had urged her to drop in there at any time. It would have been a charming social opportunity for her, had it not been for the probability of her constantly meeting Heaton and being confronted with his steady, unseeing gaze.

Then a gentler mood came to her, as she thought of him, of what he must have suffered. The blow was fresh upon him when they had first met. She could see its effect now in numberless little ways, and she marvelled to herself that he had refrained from speaking of the horror which was pursuing him and hanging over him. She wondered how it would feel to be blind. Rising, she closed her eyes and walked up and down the room; but, shut her eyes as closely as she might, she could still feel the light, and she knew that she could see it again whenever she chose. He was in the dark, the thick, black dark, and it would last forever and ever and ever.

. Something rose up in her throat and choked her, as she sprang forward impatiently and lighted the two remaining gas jets. It was unthinkable for her, this absolute darkness, and yet the thought of it terrified her. And Heaton was living like that! He had endured it for a year, and he must endure it for years to come. There was nothing left for him to do but to endure, and meet people, and talk, and smile that queer little smile of his, and make no sign. Worst of all, when she had met him, she had talked about the weather, though she knew he was watching for one accent of womanly pity. If only the evening could be lived over again, she would speak such kind, friendly words.

She went back to Idlewilde and reviewed their life there. If he remembered it at all, he must have carried away some mental picture of her. She wondered whether he still retained it, and whether he would always think of her cheeks as smarting under their coat of sunburn and her hair roughened with the lake winds. As the thought crossed her mind, she glanced into the mirror before her, and wished that she could substitute her present self, in all the splendor of her rustling silk gown. She rose wearily and began to take off her finery. The party was over, and her lesson came early in the morning. Work was work, and she must be ready for it. Arturo insisted upon regular hours, and it was Arturo who was ruling her life now, not Tom Heaton.

A week later, she called upon Mrs. Emerson; but neither at that time nor during her two succeeding calls did she see Heaton, nor did his sister make any but the most passing refer-

ence to him.   It was evident that Mrs. Emerson
had taken a fancy to the young girl, and their
intimacy grew rapidly.   The older woman had
a fashion of stopping her carriage at the door of
the boarding-house, and carrying Elinor off for
long drives or shopping tours; and before the
Christmas holidays had come, she was "Elinor"
to both Mrs. Emerson and her husband.

The friendly, informal intercourse was the best
thing possible for Elinor.   She was too busy to go
much into society, and this was the one home in
the city where she felt free to drop in at any hour
without ceremony.   It was impossible for her
to doubt the hospitality of these new friends,
and their pleasant rooms soon became nearly as
familiar to her as her own more modest quarters
at the boarding-house.   She met Heaton there
frequently.   As a rule, at the advent of callers
he retreated to his own den up-stairs; but his
sister usually sent for him whenever Elinor
appeared.

"Tom sees so few people now," she said a
little apologetically, one day; "that I like to
coax him down to take a cup of tea with us as
often as I can."

That was the nearest she had ever come to
making any reference to her brother's infirmity;
and Elinor respected her silence, the more so as
she soon discovered that, whenever Heaton was
present, his sister never lost consciousness of

him, but was always on the alert to keep him an interested sharer in the conversation.

Between Elinor and Heaton, the constraint had never entirely worn off. He was always conscious of her discomfort in his society; and Elinor, on the other hand, carried her apparent unconsciousness to the point of indifference. Once or twice, even, she had blundered into little cutting remarks which she had not realized at all until, too late, she had seen Heaton wince under them as if they had caused him physical pain.

She was sitting alone in her room, one day in December, resting after an unusually exciting hour with Arturo, when the maid brought her Heaton's card.

"There was a boy came with him," the girl explained; " but when I said you were in, the boy just came into the house with him, and went right off again and left him sitting there alone."

Heaton rose, as Elinor entered the room.

" Don't be too much surprised to see me," he said, smiling. "As a rule, I don't make calls; but I thought you'd let me drop in here, on the ground of old acquaintance, so I asked Ned to come with me."

" And where is Ned?" Elinor asked, as she drew a chair forward and sat down near her guest.

"He wanted to see a friend in the next block. The two boys are going away to school together, after the holidays, and they have a great many plans to make. He will be back here in half an hour; in the mean time, you will have to let me stay."

"It's good to have you here," she said cordially. "I was just indulging in a fit of the blues. Do you ever have them?"

"Frequently, especially of late. What was the matter; Arturo?"

"Yes, he was in a temper, to-day, and I had a bad time with him."

There was a pause. Then Heaton said suddenly, —

"I had an especial reason for coming, to-day. I wanted to be egotistic and claim the 'good boy' reward. I've been writing again, this last week."

"I'm so glad. Tell me about it. I have wondered whether you had done anything of the kind since you were at Idlewilde."

There was another pause. Heaton leaned forward in his chair, with his elbows on his knees, his face turned towards the floor.

"The fact is, Miss Tiemann," he said at length; "I wanted to see you by yourself for a while. What's the use of playing at cross purposes as we do, and talking on the surface of things? When we are together, we are both of us thinking of — this." He raised his head and turned his eyes towards her, as if to illustrate his meaning. "We may as well speak of it first as last. I know I'm not the fellow I was when you knew me at Idlewilde, and there's no use trying to hide the fact."

His voice was quiet and steady, as if he had put himself under a severe strain; but his hands gripped each other nervously. Elinor was silent, and he went on, —

"Don't think I am given to talking about it. As a rule, I let it alone; but it's a little different with you. People here got used to it by degrees; but, that first night, I knew you were taken by surprise. It's horrible to be saying this, only — can't you see? — the only way to get round it was to walk straight into the middle of it, for it kept standing in the way and spoiling all our talks."

It was painful to watch him and listen to him. Elinor felt that she could bear no more.

"Please, don't, Mr. Heaton," she said, starting up from her chair and moving a step or two away from him. "I wish you would n't say this."

He looked hurt.

"Forgive me," he said slowly. "It's an unusual thing to do, I know. Perhaps I'd better not have spoken about it, only I thought it might make it easier for you."

"It is n't that," she said half impatiently.

"Don't you know what I have wanted to say: that I am so sorry for you, so sorry for what you must have suffered, and that I wish I could do something to make it less unbearable? I wanted to tell you so; but I was — afraid."

His color came.

"Am I so changed, then? You would have said it at Idlewilde."

She dared not tell him that his blindness made the difference, that she shrank from meeting his eyes, now that the life had gone out from them. She stood looking down at him for a moment, wishing that he could read her unspoken pity and not force her to seek the right words to say. Her instinct seemed to have failed her. Under the quiet endurance to which he had trained himself, she could see that he was as sensitive as a man could be. In the coming days she would be glad that he had spoken of his trouble; but the present moment was a trying one, and it needed all her tact to meet him on his own ground. With a great effort at self-mastery, she seated herself again and said, with something of her old friendly manner, —

"It is better that we have spoken about it, even if I can't do anything but say I am sorry. I wish you would tell me all about it, all that has happened since I saw you."

"If you care to know. It's such an old story here that it seems as if every one I met had been told. It was overwork, in the first place. I had just been to an oculist when I met you, and he had told me what must come, but he could n't tell me when. I did n't feel like seeing people I knew, that summer, so Jack and I went West. Then we came home, and I waited for fourteen months. Heaven only knows how I should have gone through it, if it had n't been for Jack and my sister. They carried me along in some way; but it was a relief when it came. The waiting from one week to another, not daring to make so much as a dinner engagement without a mental reservation, was n't a pretty thing to do. Since then, I have jogged on through life at about Dexter's old pace, and found my main employment in learning to grin and bear it."

Elinor bit her lip nervously for a moment.

"How do you bear it?" she burst out. "It shuts you off from everything and leaves you alone, in spite of anything we can do. And all those days at Idlewilde you knew it was coming, and you never told us, nor let us suspect it at all."

"I never could have spoken of it," he answered steadily. "At that time, I did n't dare to think of it, even. It used to stop my breath, sometimes, and all I could do was to try to forget it. That was where you helped me so much."

"I wish I could help you now," she said impetuously.

"You have helped me more than you know. My meeting you has seemed like a link with the old days when I really lived, and it has given me pluck to go on. Besides, it has set me to writing again, and I have just finished the story I began at Idlewilde, two years ago."

"You can write, then? I'm so glad."

"After a fashion, with Bertha to help me. It makes work for her; but she is always so good to help me along. She has n't been away from me since last December, and Jack is like my other self."

There was another pause. With an effort, Elinor raised her eyes and looked steadily into the brown ones before her. They were a little expressionless and stolid; otherwise there was nothing to show that their work was done. She found it impossible to realize that Heaton was sitting there in the darkness; yet the strange, overmastering fear came back to her as she looked at him. It was as if another and a different atmosphere surrounded him, and she were powerless to enter it.

"I wish," she said slowly; "don't misunderstand me, for I mean it so truly; I wish I could do something for you. I am at your sister's so much of the time, and she never treats me like a stranger. Why could n't I —"

"It isn't anything that you can do," he replied, as he rose and, feeling for the mantel beside him, stood leaning against it. "I have been so frank that I might as well go on and tell you what I thought when I came here. If you can make up your mind to take things as they are, and not feel all the time as if you were fencing with something that you could never touch, we both shall find it easier. It is only the old problem once more: given, fate; required, the best of things."

Ned's step was heard in the hall. Elinor rose and stood beside her guest.

"I am glad that we have talked it out, Mr. Heaton," she said. "Next time we meet, it will be at the precise point where we separated at Idlewilde, and I shall expect you to give me tidings of Miss Winnie."

She followed them to the door, and stood looking after them, while Ned carefully led his companion down the strange flight of steps. Then she shut the door abruptly and, hurrying away to her room, she locked herself in and flung herself, face downward, upon the bed.

CHAPTER TEN

THE season was nearing an end and Lent was at hand. In some way or other the months had flown past, and Elinor's first year of work was more than half over. In spite of slow, monotonous toil, in spite of days of discouragement when Arturo scolded her and her voice seemed to fail her entirely, she had gone on untiringly. Since the time, more than two years before, when she had laughingly announced her intention of trying what good might be in her voice, she had never turned aside from her purpose. She rarely spoke of what that purpose might be; but, deep down in her heart, there was the dogged determination to become a singer who should deserve the name. Unfortunately for her ambition, she had long since proved that opera and its vocal pyrotechnics were out of the question for her. Whatever talent she might have, lay in other directions, and she could only hope to succeed in the field of oratorio or concert work.

At times even that seemed doubtful. It is no light matter to be the owner of a possible

voice, and Arturo was a notorious tyrant, in so
far as his pupils were concerned. They dieted,
they exercised at stated intervals, they slept at
regular hours; otherwise, they went in search
of another teacher. To all these things Elinor
gave herself up unhesitatingly. Her one choice
had been made when she selected her master;
now she was ready to rely upon his judgment
and experience, to obey his commands to the
letter. To one less enthusiastic, it would have
been a tedious time; and there were moments
when Elinor, even, was half inclined to abandon
her undertaking.

She had never supposed that one could have
as many faults as she suddenly had appeared to
develop. Her voice was improperly placed;
her breathing was bad, and her tongue was
always going astray. There are few experiences
more humiliating than to practise, day after day,
with one's eyes fixed upon a mirror set up to
serve as a detective, so far as one's faults are
concerned. One loses mental perspective, and
the tongue becomes hideously prominent.
However, Elinor toiled on, rewarded by an
occasional nod of approval from her teacher,
and she soon learned that his gruff " Go on "
was the highest praise for which she could
hope.

" Still," he remarked, one day, resting his
elbows on the piano, and screwing himself

around to look at her; "you are better than I had thought, signorina. You were very bad indeed for a long time. Do not think you are good now," he added hastily. "There is much for you to unlearn yet, but there is a certain purity of tone which says to me that I must not dismay. Time will do much, and patience will do more. No?"

"But when can I begin to sing?" she asked a little wearily. "It seems to me that I have done nothing yet."

He shrugged his shoulders.

"Ah, you are tired. You must not be. I am never, never tired and I am but one, while there are many of you. You cannot make a singer in a day, and you can never make a singer unless you have the three gifts: the voice, the ear, and the musical passion. You have the ear, and I shall try to make the voice; but the musical passion must come of itself. You sing now as if you were made of bones, not blood. To sing, you must have lived. And even that is not enough; you must have lived outside of your own life. A music box is very soothing; but it can never stir us till the tears fall. That is what a singer must do, signorina. To sing, that is to have a mission, and you must undertake it with conviction and, above all, with reverence."

His little dark eyes were not fixed upon her; but were gazing thoughtfully beyond, as if

7

towards the far-away source of all music. For the moment, his round, chubby face was transfigured; then abruptly he returned to the present time and place.

" Now, once again ! " he exclaimed. " Now! *Boum, boum, ta ta ta ta ta ta, tum, pom, pa-a-am!* Ah, you are too late! Here am I singing all the brasses and everything, and when I get there, you don't do anything, you know. You should feel the music, and then you would be ready. Let us don't lose any more time, and remember to pray very sweetly, to get what you want. Open the mouth wide, so that the sound can come forth. Ah-h-h-h! You are forgetting the tongue."

"To think," Elinor said to Heaton, that night; " that singing like this depends upon such details! Fancy Elsa being scolded about her tongue, and practising her high notes in front of a mirror! I suppose that is what they all have to go through; but we don't realize it."

" Shakespeare had to learn to spell," he was beginning, with a smile, when Elinor interrupted him.

" No, he didn't; at least, not very thoroughly, and that Ortrud didn't learn to sing. Still, exceptions appear to prove the rule, and we belong to the unhappy majority who have to learn the *A, B, C,* of our trade. But tell me, are you still writing?"

"Now and then a little. It's much harder work now, you know; and it isn't often I'm feeling like it. My Idlewilde story will be out, next week. May I send it to you?"

"Of course. I always like to see what my friends are doing, and this is peculiarly my story, you know, as long as I prompted you to finish it. Why not read it to me, some day, before it comes out?"

She had made the remark carelessly, for her attention had been distracted for the moment. Too late she saw her mistake, as Heaton answered briefly, —

"You are demanding the impossible, Miss Tiemann. I can type my stories with the average amount of correctness; but then I have to wait for some one to read them over to me, on approval."

"I wish I could be the some one," she answered gently. "It must be a treat to read a new story before the author himself has done it. Most of us have to wait until the freshness is quite worn off. There goes the curtain."

She had found a note awaiting her, on her return from her lesson, saying that Mr. Emerson had had the offer of a box at the opera, that night, and asking her to dine and go with them. Elinor had promptly accepted the invitation, and she had so much enjoyed the cosy little dinner alone with the Emersons and Heaton that she had been almost sorry when the carriage was announced.

At the close of the first act, she had risen, and, leaving the Emersons who were busy in recognizing their friends scattered through the house, she had moved to the back of the box where Heaton had been sitting alone.

"Is it satisfactory?" he asked, as she sat down at his side.

"Perfect," she answered, with a sigh of content. "You know I 've never heard 'Lohengrin' before. I have been brought up on Italian opera, and this is a revelation to me."

"How is the setting? Good?"

"Beyond criticism; or, at least, I 'm not in a critical mood. If you could only see it all, and enjoy it with us! It makes me feel deplorably selfish to have so much more than my share."

"What 's the use?" he asked. "At least, I can hear it, and that is something to be thankful for. Some day, I hope I am going to hear you. I never heard you sing but once, that night in the boat. Do you remember?"

Elinor nodded. Then, recollecting herself, she said, —

"I remember. 'T was the night we went to the hop; was n't it? I sang the little Kücken 'Schlummerlied.' I hope I can do better than that now, though Arturo might tell a different story, I am afraid."

"By the way, have you ever run across Jack, there at the studio?"

"Mr. Wyckoff? No. Is he a fellow-sufferer there?"

"Didn't you know it? He has a good voice, and he has studied with Arturo for a long time."

"Remember that Jack, as you call him, is still a myth to me. I have never seen him, in spite of the numberless times we have just missed each other, and I begin to have serious doubts of his existence. What is he like, anyway?"

"He used to be a wonderfully handsome fellow, and they say he hasn't changed much. I always think of him as he looked, the last time he dined here before my eyes gave out. He was in full panoply, for he was going on to some other places. I never saw him brighter nor more stunning, and I never saw him again. He came to see me, two days later; but it was too late."

"Was it as sudden as that?" Elinor asked in a lower voice.

"Yes; it doesn't take long, under some circumstances. I read the 'Rubaiyát,' that morning. I used to live on it, in those days. But this is a very inappropriate subject, Miss Tiemann. You were asking about Jack. He is a fellow that everybody likes; there probably isn't a more popular man in the city. He is a

sort of a hero of mine, in a way, for he is succeeding in all the things that I used to try for.
I don't envy him, though; he deserves his luck,
if only for the way he has stood by me. I want
you to meet him, and I wonder that you have n't
done it, long ago. He is at the house, almost
every day."

The curtain rose just then, and, with a word
of apology, Elinor left him and moved forward
to join the others.

Later on in the evening, several friends of the
Emersons had dropped in to see them, and the
talk had been the impersonal gossip of the hour
and the place. In the interval before the last
act, however, Mrs. Emerson had joined her
brother at the back of the box, leaving Mr.
Emerson to entertain their guest. Suddenly
Elinor turned to her companion.

"Do you know," she said abruptly; "how
Mr. Heaton's blindness changes things?"

"How do you mean?" Mr. Emerson asked.
"I don't quite understand."

"I don't, myself," she answered, while a little
troubled look came into her eyes. "Even in
the little time we used to know each other, we
were such good friends; and now I seem to say
the wrong thing to him so often. I'm so sorry
for him, and I like him so much; but I am continually making mistakes when I am with him.
I don't realize where I am going until the mis-

chief is done, and then it's too late, for I can't apologize. I wish we could get back on the old ground; but it appears to be impossible."

"Poor Tom!" said Mr. Emerson gravely. "I know how it is with you. He generally shuts his teeth and goes through his bad times by himself; but it has been a terrible blow to him, this giving up all his plans, and it has left him sensitive and sore all over. Bertha and Wyckoff are the only ones who know just how to manage him, and they never make mistakes. There's Wyckoff now," he added, as the door of the box opened.

Elinor turned around, curious to see the cousin of whom she had heard so much. He was bending over the sofa on which the brother and sister were lounging, and something in his bright blue eyes and his tall figure struck her as being familiar; but she studied him in vain, at a loss to discover the secret of the puzzling resemblance. He glanced once or twice at Elinor; but he lingered at Heaton's side, laughing and talking with his cousins. It was impossible for Elinor to overhear their conversation; but, as she stealthily watched them, she was astonished at the change in Heaton's face and manner. For the moment he had lost his older, saddened look, and his face was bright and boyish again as she had not seen it since they parted, three years before.

Wyckoff remained at his side until the curtain rose for the last time. Then, arm in arm, they came forward. A moment later, he had been introduced to Elinor and had dropped into the chair between herself and Heaton. In the interest of the climax of the opera, conversation was abandoned, and it was not until the curtain fell that Elinor had the opportunity to exchange more than an occasional word with him. As they left the box, however, on their way to the carriage, he placed himself at her side.

"I am beginning to feel slightly hurt, Miss Tiemann," he said laughingly, while he threw her cloak about her shoulders. "We have met before, and yet you obstinately refuse to accept me as an old acquaintance."

"But I'm sure we did n't meet," she answered. "You had left Idlewilde before I knew Mr. Heaton, and we had gone before you came back. You may have seen me there; but I know we have never spoken to each other till to-night."

"Alas for your memory!" he said. "I was under the distinct impression that I had not only talked with you, but that I had taken a short ride with you, once upon a time."

She looked up at him incredulously.

"Where?"

"Here in New York."

"I know you are mistaken, Mr. Wyckoff. I wonder whom you have mixed up with me. I assure you, it's not at all flattering to my vanity to have you so uncertain about your companions."

"Nor to mine to have you forget me so completely," he replied. "I do remember seeing you at Idlewilde, before I went away; but you appear to have forgotten the day you called Arturo a little monster."

She laughed aloud, such a gay little laugh, that Heaton, just behind, raised his head to listen.

"Are you the unhappy man who was taking a lesson? I was sorry for you then, even if I did n't say so. Experience has only served to increase my sympathy for you. But what was the ride?"

"In the elevator, of course. I can't say that I enjoyed it, for you did n't appear to be in a happy frame of mind, and you scowled at me as darkly as if I had been Arturo himself. You are really studying with him, then?"

"Yes; at least, I spend two hours a week in being maltreated by him. I knew that you were one of his pupils. Mr. Heaton was just speaking of it; but I never thought to connect you with the tenor I heard, that first day. You see, you were nothing but a voice then, a mere abstraction."

"Let us hope that, in time, I may become something more concrete," he returned gayly, as he put her into the carriage. "I say, Tom," he added, while he helped his cousin to his seat; "I'm coming up, to-morrow, to get you to go down to the Philharmonic with me. Perhaps, if I am very good, Miss Tiemann will let you take me to call on her, some day. Good night." He raised his hat, and was lost in the crowd.

CHAPTER ELEVEN

By the middle of May, the Emersons were settled in their summer home, in one of the suburban towns overlooking the Sound. For the past year or two, they had gone out of town earlier than usual, partly for the sake of baby Ruth, who was never as well in the city, partly on Heaton's account. Since his blindness, the social life of the town had become painful to him, although it had been impossible for him to escape from it entirely. He had never been a society man, in the fullest sense of the term, and he had submitted rather impatiently to the efforts of his friends to make a lion of him. It was as Elinor had said, three years before. His cousin and his sister drew him into their round of gayety; but he had been best content when he could step aside and watch the procession as it swept past him. He had been looked up to and admired; he had been a popular man in a way, but it was a popularity mingled with a little feeling of awe, and not at all like that inspired by his more approachable cousin.

Then his blindness had come and put an end to it all. Until then, Heaton had never realized

EACH LIFE UNFULFILLED

how much he had enjoyed his social success.
It had been easy to disdain it; but when he
was forced to step to one side and become a
passive listener, it suddenly grew desirable again.
Left to himself, he would have shut himself
away from the world; but his sister was too wise
to allow that, and she usually succeeded in coax-
ing him to put in a tardy appearance at most
of the dinners and receptions which she gave.
More than that she could not do. Heaton quietly
declined to go out with her, and she was forced
to content herself with this compromise.

Strange to say, he had found that his mascu-
line friends had been more loyal to him than
the women by whom he had formerly been so
graciously received. In his more bitter moods,
he attributed this to the fact of his uselessness
from a social point of view. The man who
could neither act as escort, dance, nor forage
at a crowded table, he reasoned, had no right to
exist. He should move to one side, to make
room for his more utilitarian brethren. The
fact was, however, that the cause lay in the isolation of his blindness, in the vague discomfort
which it roused in the people before him. The
women he had known earlier in his life, who
had danced with him and talked to him in dimly-
lighted conservatories, now stood aloof and
watched him in silent pity, powerless to think
of a word to say to him.

108

"There's poor Tom Heaton, sitting alone over there in the corner," they were accustomed to whisper to each other. "I wonder if he'd be hurt, if I offered to sit out a dance with him."

But they never did sit out a dance with him; and little by little their acquaintance with him had almost come to an end. It was better that it should, Heaton felt. In their occasional conversations, he had been quick to realize the embarrassment of which he was the cause, and it had rendered their intercourse a painful ordeal on both sides.

That was during the first winter, when his trouble was fresh upon him, while, quite as fresh in all their minds, there was the recollection of what he formerly had been. By the second season, it had come to be a recognized fact that he should lurk in the background, and find his sole variety in the companionship of his men friends, who rarely failed to seek him out for a few moments before the evening was over.

In all this experience, Elinor had been the one exception. In spite of her first evening of discomfort with him, in spite of the fact that she too shared the general feeling of awe which he called up, she had proved a loyal friend. Her position as a privileged guest of the house had made her able to disregard the conventional prejudice which forbade her companions to go to the man who could not go to them. She

had gone to his side repeatedly, when she had
seen him deserted, and she had never failed to
find a welcome. To be sure, the conversation
had frequently languished, and they both had
been conscious of points of danger which had
been avoided only with difficulty; but, after all,
Heaton had come to rely upon her companionship for at least a part of every evening they
were together, and he quickly learned to anticipate her bright chatter, which formed an enjoyable contrast to the more ponderous conversation
of the men.

Long before the season was ended, their companionship had ripened into a sort of intimacy.
They had liked each other from the first moment
of their meeting; their tastes were allied, for
music and literature must always go hand in
hand. Even the little feeling of remoteness
between them was fast dying away. For this,
Heaton was largely responsible. Since the day
of his first mentioning his blindness to Elinor,
he had never avoided the subject; but he had
alluded to it in a matter-of-course tone which
had restored much of their old friendly freedom.
When the subject had to be mentioned, they
accepted it as a fact, and spoke of it without
reserve; otherwise they disregarded it entirely,
as being an insignificant detail which in no way
affected their friendly relations. All this was
inexpressibly comforting to Heaton. As a rule,

he was constantly annoyed by the cold neglect
or the elaborate attentions of his companions;
and Elinor's off-hand way of looking out for
his comfort was as soothing as it was unusual.

Arturo had been called to Boston, for a week
at Easter, and Elinor had taken advantage of the
temporary break in her work, to spend the time
with the Emersons. There she and Heaton had
been continually together, often alone, for Mrs.
Emerson was a mother of the old-fashioned
type, and gave several hours of each day to
little Ruth. Under these circumstances, their
friendship ripened rapidly. Elinor had been
tireless in her attentions to Heaton, singing and
reading aloud to him, or discussing his work with
him, all in a careless, good-natured way which
made it impossible for him to feel any lasting
sense of indebtedness.

She had no wish that he should feel it. She
liked Heaton sincerely, and she always enjoyed
meeting him and talking with him. In her New
York life, she had found no one who was more
congenial to her; and yet, strange to say, in all
this increasing intimacy, she had never thought
of him as anything but a friend. If she had
stopped to analyze her impressions, she would
have told herself that it was impossible for him
to be anything else. Other men she could meet
and contemplate, in time, as possible lovers; but
Heaton seemed to her to be shut off from all

that side of life. His blindness had ended that for him. He was as far removed from all questions of love as he was from reading the daily papers to her. For this reason, there was nothing unconventional, to her mind, in their friendship. It was just friendship, nothing more; and it was as such that she enjoyed it.

She was sitting on the Emersons' piazza, one night in June, watching the twilight creep over the lawn and over the blue Sound which stretched away beyond. Since they had left the city for the season, she had seen her friends much less often. It had been impossible for her to take the time from her work to run out of town for the frequent calls which she had been accustomed to make, when they were within a few blocks of her. She had missed them constantly, and the warm days of early summer were beginning to wear upon her. She was tired of the noise and hurry of the city; she was sick of the glare of the baked pavements and of the smell of the dusty streets. It had been a relief to turn her back upon them, even for a few hours, and to enjoy the quiet country home and the congenial atmosphere of the dinner-table.

After dinner, Mr. Emerson had gone to his evening paper and his evening cigar, and Mrs. Emerson had excused herself for a few moments, to give some necessary orders to her maids.

Elinor sat quiet for a little while after she went away. Then she started up.

"Mr. Heaton, I must go out on the lawn. It is so long since I have walked on any grass that I want to see how it feels. Don't come with me unless you like; but I really can't sit still any longer."

He had already risen, and he fell into step at her side, as she moved off across the lawn which sloped gently down to the water's edge. Inside the house, his step was firmer; but here it was a little uncertain. Elinor hesitated for a moment; then she tucked her hand through his arm.

"It makes it easier to keep in step," she said apologetically. "But you don't know how good it is to feel the country around me again. I begin to rejoice that I am going home in ten days."

"So soon as that?"

She was surprised at the note of regret in his voice.

"Yes, I shall be through with my lessons on the twentieth, and I shall start for home, the next day."

"But you are coming back?"

"I'm not sure. It all depends on Arturo. If he is no more encouraging than he has been for the last month, I may give up. But I want to tell you; I read your 'Wheels within Wheels,' the other day."

8   113

"How did you like it?" he asked quickly, for he had come to depend upon talking over his work with her.

"It is your best work yet," she said, with a frankness which bore no taint of flattery. "It is more logical; but it is so pitiless. I confess to a few tears over the ending, even if it was the one inevitable result."

He smiled.

"I think I must have rather a genius for the pathetic. I don't start for it at all; but my characters always come to some untimely end, instead of rioting properly."

"Are you doing anything now?" she asked, as they paused at the water's edge, and stood listening to the little waves that crawled up across the sand.

"No; I mean to rest and do nothing, all summer long. It's warm work, wallowing in woe, with the thermometer in the nineties. Besides, there's Bertha, you know. I don't like to make her work so much."

"Does she do much of it?" Elinor asked. "Forgive me if I seem inquisitive; but I've often wondered how much you can do, yourself."

"Only a little. One of the first things I did, after I knew my eyes were going to give out, was to learn to use a typewriter. I can do that fairly well; but of course I can't read over what I have written, and I get into a hopeless tangle, every now and then. My manuscripts are strange-looking things when they go into Bertha's hands; but she generally contrives to puzzle them out and put them in order."

"Isn't there some other kind of a way you could write?" she said slowly. It was a question she had often longed to put, yet now she shrank from it.

"How do you mean?"

"I thought there was an alphabet you could learn to write and then to read over what you had written. Wouldn't it be a help?" she asked bravely, though her hand shook a little, as it rested on his arm.

The idea seemed to please him.

"I remember now, — Braille, isn't it? I remember hearing something about it, years ago, before I ever thought I could have any personal interest in it. I'm glad you spoke of it. There must be places in town where they teach it, and I'll take it up, in the fall. It's only a question of my touch. That isn't acute at all, you see, and even my typewriter troubles me sometimes. I suppose it is one of the disadvantages of growing blind so late in life."

"Your touch can be trained; can't it?" she said. "I — we all want you to do everything that makes it easier for you to write, for we must have your stories, no matter how much work they make for you. And you enjoy it, yourself, don't you?"

"Yes," he replied thoughtfully; "and no. When I am writing and it all goes well, I think there's nothing better; but when the mood passes, I am always disgusted to find that it really amounts to so little."

"I suppose that is the fate of us all," Elinor responded, and there was a little tone of despondency in her words. "Even perfect success has its disappointments. My own dream never will be fulfilled; but, even if it were, I should probably find it no more satisfactory than any other air-castle."

"What is the dream?" he asked curiously. "Or don't you like to tell it?"

"To sing," she answered earnestly; "to sing just once in public, to satisfy myself. I'd work, and slave, and starve, even, for the sake of accomplishing it. But Arturo says it's no use, that I haven't the ability, and that I am too cold to be an artist, a real musician. I am afraid he is right; but still I keep on hoping and working. I try to believe your old creed you quoted at Idlewilde; but I am afraid my only satisfaction will have to come from my work, not from the success that ought to follow."

"Let the success take care of itself," he said gravely. "The work is all that counts for much, and there's nothing better, after all. Work for work's sake is the real thing. When your reputation is an established fact, you will look back to this very year, and think that you had the best of life then, and that the best day of the year was the day you were working hardest to get to the ideal before you."

There was a short silence. Then Elinor turned to him impulsively.

"Thank you, Mr. Heaton; I believe you are right. This isn't the first time that you have given me the courage to go on with my work. I only wish I could help you as much."

"You have," he answered humbly; "more than you will ever know."

CHAPTER TWELVE

It was the evening of the fourth of July, nearly a month after Elinor's last call at the Emersons'. Heaton was lying in the hammock at the end of the piazza, and Mr. and Mrs. Emerson were sitting on the steps, watching the rockets as they shot up from the distant city. A strong south wind was blowing up from the water, and across the lawn they could hear the regular beating of the waves upon the sand, while, far away to the south, a faint line of light showed the rising moon.

At length, Mr. Emerson broke the silence.

" I had a letter from Gray, this morning, and it is all settled that we are to have the cottage by the first of August. Can you be ready?"

" Of course. I 'll be ready at a day's notice," Mrs. Emerson replied promptly. " Which cottage is it?"

" The furnished one up by the hotel. Mrs. Gray wants us to let her maids stay there while she is at the shore, so all you will have to do will be to make out a list of the provisions you need to have ordered, and to pack our trunks."

"Jack is talking of spending a week at the hotel while we are there," Mrs. Emerson said, as she made room for her son to seat himself on the step below her. "I tried to make him think that it would be pleasanter for him at the cottage; but he insisted that he wanted the freedom of hotel life. How much room is there in the cottage?"

"All we need, and more too," answered her husband, as he lighted his cigar. "Let's have somebody to stay with us. We may as well fill the house."

"I was thinking of that. What do you say to my writing to ask Elinor Tiemann to come to us? I think she has no settled plans for August, and she always seems to fit into the family as if she belonged there. What do you think about it, Tom?"

"What's that?" he asked, rolling himself out of the hammock and going to join the group on the steps.

"Of my asking Elinor to spend August with us," she repeated. "Edwin has heard that we can have the Grays' cottage, and now we want somebody to fill it."

"You know I always like Miss Tiemann," he answered. "Have you heard from her, since she went away?"

"Only once, the letter I read you. I was a little surprised at her going away without

coming out here again to say good-by. I saw
her in town, one morning, and told her to be
sure to come out and lunch with us."

"Miss Tiemann always does have a winsome
fashion of suiting her own convenience, first of
all," Ned remarked, with the little tone of conscious superiority which six months of boarding-
school life can develop in the least conceited
of boys.

His uncle laughed.

"On what do you base your theory, Ned?"
he inquired. "You had seen her just twice
when you went away; and I think you have n't
seen her at all since you came home again."

"I don't know," the boy answered, as he
leaned back and rested his arm across his
uncle's knee. "She seems kind of slippery,
somehow, and I think she 'll be no addition to
our fun at the lake. If Cousin Jack goes up,
she 'll take all of his time, see if she does n't;
and I sha' n't be in it at all."

A slight expression of annoyance crossed
Heaton's face. Till that moment, he had not
realized that his cousin was to be within reach
of the cottage. He had been counting upon
having Elinor's society for himself, upon dropping back into the old life they had known at
Idlewilde.

"I think I rather agree with Ned," Mr. Emerson said thoughtfully. "Elinor is amazingly

superficial, and I think it would be impossible for her to feel anything very deeply. She is a child in character. Still, she is a bright, attractive little thing, and always good company, and there's nobody I would like better to have staying with us, Bertha. Is she coming back to New York, next year?"

"I think so. Arturo advises it; but he refuses to promise anything for her future. She isn't a child in the determination she has shown about her singing. Even you must admit that, Edwin."

"I do admit it, my dear," he said, as he rose; "and she certainly deserves to succeed. I'm not slandering Elinor; I am only making a critical analysis of her character. She's all there, only she needs something to develop her. She may find it, this very summer. Come, my scholastic son, come out and take your old father rowing, and leave your mother to write to Miss Tiemann. Tell her to be there by the third, Bertha. Then, if she comes back for another year, we can all come down together."

"I think Edwin doesn't quite do Elinor justice," Mrs. Emerson said, after her husband had left them. "She's only an undeveloped child; but I am very fond of her, and I think she is good for us all."

"She certainly is good to me," Heaton said

thoughtfully. "She is the only woman left now, except you, that ever has a word to say to me."

"I'm glad you enjoy her, Tom. I think that she is fond of you, too. Not that she's in love with you," she added, with a little laugh. "Elinor isn't given to sentiment; but I know she always enjoys seeing you and talking things over with you."

The moon had come up above the horizon, and its pale light lay across the water and the lawn, and fell full upon Heaton's face. At her last words, Mrs. Emerson could see a sudden compression of her brother's lips. Then he said briefly, —

"She must. I only hope she appreciates the privilege. But I want to go up to finish my story." And he rose.

"Oh, don't, Tom," his sister urged, surprised at his sudden change of tone. "It's too late to work, to-night, and I am all alone here. Stay with me."

"I can't, Bertha," he replied more gently. "I'm in the mood for working now, and I'd better try it."

Unable to read his mood, and only seeing that something had hurt him more than she had at first realized, she stretched out her hand to his for a moment. Then she said brightly, —

"Go, then, and inspiration be on your pen!

I will write a note to Elinor. Have you any message?"

"No; I think not. No; not any," he said, as he turned away.

His face was in shadow now, and his sister could not see the little quiver of his lip. She followed him into the house and up to his den, to assure herself that everything was in order for his work. As she went down-stairs to her own desk, she heard the door close behind her.

The room was flooded with the silvery light which came in at the two open windows, stole across the floor, and rested upon the great writing-table covered with papers and the appliances for his work. Heaton took one or two quick turns up and down the room. Then, instead of sitting down at his table and going on with his half-finished story, he threw himself on the broad couch by the window and buried his face in his hands.

In spite of his determination to do no work through the summer, for days his new story had been absorbing all his interest. He had felt sure that this was to be his best effort, and he had worked at it with an almost feverish intensity of purpose. Now, all at once, he saw that it was only a string of empty words in comparison with the real story in the midst of which he was living.

At his sister's careless words, the truth had burst upon him in an instant, though he knew now that it had been coming to him for weeks and months, and that unconsciously he had put it away from him, as something in which he could have no share. For the past three or four years, ever since his blindness had first threatened him, he had been trying to reconcile himself to the thought that love must never enter into his life, that he had no right to offer a woman what, at best, could be only a partial gift. He had supposed he had learned his lesson. He had supposed that he was enjoying Elinor only as her own brother might have done. Now, all at once and too late, he recognized his mistake.

And this, then, was love! His lip curled scornfully, as he recalled the day when, beside the brook, he had told Elinor that he lacked the necessary experience to write a novel. The experience had come to him now, and in all its bitterness, for he could never tell her his love and ask her to share his imperfect life. How long had he loved her? Did she care for him? He must think it all out.

His brain was throbbing. His hands, clasped over his eyes, could feel the jar of the blood pulsing across his temples. The room seemed suffocating to him; and he started up and began to pace the floor again. Then he dropped into a chair by the open window, and rested his face against the cool wood of the casing.

It had been going on for weeks and weeks, during all that winter of frequent and informal meetings. He recalled a thousand and one little circumstances of their acquaintance, of the days they had spent at Idlewilde, of his first call upon her in New York, of their countless friendly talks. She had been so thoughtful of his comfort, had shown such tact in her little womanly attentions. His sister, even, had not been kinder to him. And yet she had hurt him often with the inconsiderate words which had stung him to the quick. Still, from her they had not caused him half the pain they would have done from the lips of another woman; and now, in the days that had followed her going away, he would have been glad of even the hurt. The loneliness was the hardest of it all to bear.

For one moment, he half resolved to write to her, to tell her the whole story and try to win her love, as another man would have done in his place. Then his whole nature recoiled from the temptation. He could offer her a home and all the luxuries which money could buy; he could offer her all the love which a man could bestow upon a woman; but it would be coupled with a demand for constant care and attention which would burden her young womanhood and darken her whole life. She could only marry him out of pity, and he would never consent to ask for and accept so great a sacrifice. No; he must go through it alone and make no sign.

That would be the hardest part of it all, to be thrown with her constantly, to have to keep up the same old relations of pleasant friendship, and never allow her to read the secret of his love. If he had been the hero of one of his own stories, he could have cried for his own sorrow. As it was, he could only summon all his manliness and grind his teeth together, to make no sound which could tell of his pain. With a dull feeling of pity for himself, his mind went back to the early days of his blindness. He had always supposed that life could offer him no more bitter sorrow than he had known at that time; but it was so slight, in comparison with the present. He had been able almost to forget his blindness, when he was with Elinor. If only they could have spent their lives together, the rest would have made little difference.

All at once, he raised his head abruptly. What was the use of cringing like a beaten hound? Life was before him, teaching him one of the hardest of its lessons. He was no coward; he must learn it like a man. He would never throw himself upon the generosity of a young girl, and spoil the brilliant career for which she was working. Let him think what to do first.

After all, there was nothing to do. That was the worst of it. He must go on in precisely the old way, hiding his secret from them all. Next month, they would be together again. He tried to think of some excuse which he could offer for his absence; but he knew that it would only break up the plan. It was on his account that the Emersons had chosen the quiet little mountain lake where he could have more freedom than at a larger resort. He must go with them, at whatever cost to himself. In the mean time, he could be teaching himself to forget. Perhaps he could even find out his mistake, and learn that this, after all, was not love.

But, down in his secret heart, he knew that it was all true, that he loved Elinor Tiemann as only a strong man can love the one woman of his choice, and that, for her sake, he must conquer his love. His head fell forward again upon his clasped hands, and he remained there motionless while the moon rode up across the cloudless sky, until it left him sitting in deep shadow.

At last, he rose with an effort, crossed the room to the table, and took up the finished sheets of his story. Impatiently he tore them across and began a new page. Great drops of moisture gathered on his face, for the room was warm, and he was exhausted with his struggle; but his one chance of forgetfulness lay in his work, and he turned to it, as by instinct. Hour after hour he wrote on, regardless of the striking of the little clock by his side; and the first light of the new day found him still at his self-appointed task.

CHAPTER THIRTEEN

THE first week in August saw Elinor established in the Emersons' cottage at the lake. She had needed little urging to make her consent to the plan. Mrs. Mackie was going abroad with her husband, and their usual month at the mountains had been given up on that account. Elinor had been trying to resign herself to a prolonged summer at Idlewilde, when Mrs. Emerson's letter had reached her.

She had been warmly welcomed, when she had reached the cottage, tired and dusty from her three days' ride. Ned himself forgot his prejudice when she came down to supper, that night, for a long nap and a fresh white gown had worked a wonderful change in her appearance, and even a critical youth of sixteen is not proof against the charms of a pretty woman.

Heaton had been invisible until they met at the door of the dining-room. As Elinor stepped forward to greet him, she was struck by the change in his face.

" Have you been ill, Mr. Heaton? " she asked, as she took his hand.

"Ill? Oh, no," he answered quickly. "What should make you think so?"

"I thought you did n't look quite as well as when I saw you last," she returned. "You have probably been overworking, instead of taking the rest you promised yourself. What's the story?"

"I am afraid my last story would n't prove interesting to you. It has been taking all my time lately to work it out, and now it's not likely to be a pleasant one for anybody."

"I don't believe it," she answered, as she seated herself in her usual place beside him at the table. "Anyway, you have done your last work for a month to come. We are all going to live out of doors here and be lazy; are n't we, Bertha? You see if it does n't carry you back to the old days at Idlewilde, Mr. Heaton. I have several messages to you from the natives. Nobody there appears to regard it as at all strange that we have met. They look at New York from the point of view of Idlewilde, and Mrs. Rose is quite disappointed that I don't know her aunt, Mrs. Smith, who lives somewhere near Broadway."

The days that followed were far too short for their enjoyment. Elinor and Wyckoff were often together, for Jack had taken up his abode at the hotel, on the day after her coming to the cottage. While the others went around and around the lake in the little steamers, they used to step into one of the small boats at the landing and row away across the water to the fishing grounds at the east side of the lake. Ned was usually with them. He preferred the smaller boat and the chance of an occasional fish, and he took infinite satisfaction in the deferential way in which Elinor consulted his opinion and allowed him to carry her sun umbrella.

Then there were the merry evenings on the piazza, or an occasional stroll over to the hotel to call on their new friends. Still more rarely there was a long rainy day when they remained housed, idly talking, or reading aloud, or watching the flurries of wind sweep over the lake and the floating clouds rise and fall over Mount Kearsarge and the more distant blue peaks beyond.

To Heaton alone the days were not all pleasant. He kept his secret well, and did his best to appear his usual self. For the most part, he succeeded. They all wondered a little at the occasional irritability from which he had always before been so free; but they only attributed it to his sensitiveness in meeting so many strangers, and they were quick to pardon it, though without a thought of the constant strain to which he was subjecting himself.

He was only human, and often, in spite of his

resolutions, he gave himself up unreservedly to the delight of his long hours with Elinor. She had never been brighter nor more agreeable than during those days at the cottage. She was more considerate of him, too, for down in her secret heart she reproached herself for the constant contrast she was mentally making between him and Wyckoff, whose never-failing activity and exuberant spirits rendered him a most enjoyable companion for her. She was unremitting in all her little attentions to Heaton; but, strange to say, for the first time in their intercourse it hurt him to receive these attentions. They only seemed to him to emphazise the gulf between them, the hopelessness of his hopes.

Often, when he was left alone, he went back to the memory of that other lake where he and Elinor had met, three years before. In a way they were repeating their old experience, in this lazy summer life; yet for him it was all so changed. At Idlewilde he had been the leader, the one to take the initiative, as a man should do; here he could only follow the others. There he had so often rowed Elinor back and forth across the lake; here he was only so much useless ballast, and, when they went out together, it was Elinor who did the rowing. The parallelism quickly ceased; but nevertheless it was there, and it hurt him.

Elinor never realized the envy with which Heaton stood by, while she started off with his cousin for their daily walk or row; but something in her mood, when she returned, led her to devote the remaining hours of the day to him. It was not that she was entirely unselfish in the matter, either. The two men were so perfectly contrasted, that, after an hour or two of Wyckoff's quick, flashing talk, there was a certain restfulness in escaping to Heaton once more. With Jack she was merely the light, bright summer girl with scarcely a thought beyond the present hour; but when she left him for Heaton, life became more earnest, her hopes and purposes stronger.

Wyckoff's week had gradually lengthened into two, and the last Saturday evening of his stay had come. It had been a stormy day; but towards night it had cleared, and he had walked over to the cottage in company with a pretty Miss Whitney who had met Elinor, a few years before, and who had lost no opportunity of renewing the acquaintance.

"What a glorious evening!" Elinor said, as they sat on the broad piazza overlooking the lake. "This is Mr. Wyckoff's last available night here, — we're all to go to the hotel, to-morrow night, — so why not go out for one last row together? You can take Mr. Heaton and me, Ned; and Mr. Wyckoff can row Bertha and

Miss Whitney," she added, with a naughty satisfaction in Jack's energetic demonstrations of dissent.

Fifteen minutes later, they were gliding away across the lake. It was not in vain that Wyckoff had been stroke on his college crew, and his boat soon shot far ahead of the other and was lost in the shadows of the southern shore. Elinor and Ned rowed lazily out into the middle of the lake; then Elinor dropped her oars.

"Let's lie here and rock, for a few minutes," she said. "The others don't seem to be socially inclined, and these little waves in the moonlight are too pretty to leave. Or do you prefer to keep moving, Mr. Heaton?"

"As you like," he answered, while he pocketed his little cloth cap and folded his hands at the back of his head.

From the clear sky above the heights of Mount Eyrie, the moon was shining directly down upon his face, upturned as if he could feel its radiance; and his expression appeared to have caught something of its serenity. For the moment, he was quite content. He could feel the quiet beauty of the night about him; he could hear the distant cries of the night birds along the shore, and the dreamy plash of the water as it lapped the sides of the boat. Ned, lounging in the bow, was forgotten, and the rest of the world were far away. Only he and

Elinor were there, just as they had been upon
that other night. Even now he could see the
low hills about them, the rosy glow in the west.
If it all had only come earlier, when he had the
right to love her, and to tell her of his love!
No matter then if blindness had followed, as
long as she was already his. Now the insur-
mountable barrier had risen up between them.
He could only stand aside and leave her with
his cousin.

But to-night even his cousin was not there;
just they two, rocking on the lake. He could
feel the folds of her skirt as they fell across his
foot; and once, when she bent forward to dip
her fingers in the cool water, the wind blew a
stray lock of her hair across his fingers as they
lay on the edge of the boat. The touch seemed
to run up his arm in little pricking lines, and
he longed just once to lay his hand on her soft,
fluffy hair. But he clasped his hands at the
back of his head once more and turned away,
although he felt sure that she was watching him,
startled at his quick change of position.

"I am afraid you are tired," she said. "I
forgot that you can't enjoy it as I do."

Involuntarily he bit his lip and gave his mustache a little impatient jerk. At least, there
was no need to remind him of the fact. If he
could forget and be so contented, why could
she not let him have his one short hour?

"Perhaps I may enjoy it more than you know," he said curtly. "However, don't let me keep you, if you are anxious to get back to the others — and Jack," he longed to add; but he was too much the gentleman for that.

It was the first time he had used this tone to her, and Elinor was more hurt than she cared to admit. She merely nodded to Ned, and took up her own oars again; but she scarcely spoke while they were rowing back to the shore. At the landing, they were overtaken by the other boat; and, as they stepped up on the little pier, she abruptly walked away with Jack and Miss Whitney, leaving the others to follow as they would. Later, when they were all on the steps of the cottage, saying good night, there was a slight additional cordiality in her manner to his cousin, which Heaton was quick to feel as an intentional reproach to himself.

The next evening, according to their promise, they all went over to the hotel. For an hour they sat outside, watching the twilight darken over the lake. Then some one had suggested music, and they had gone to the parlor, which quickly filled with the idlers whom the fact of its being Sunday night had debarred from more exciting pleasures. There were a few feeble choruses; then, after the capabilities of " Coronation " and " How Can I Bear to Leave Thee " had been exhausted, the amateurs had preferred to lapse into silence, and Elinor and Wyckoff were left to sing some of Mendelssohn's familiar duets. During the past few weeks they had often sung together, and their voices blended well, Jack's making up in expression for Elinor's greater power and brilliancy. Each time they paused, there was an instant demand for another song; so they had gone on, giving one old favorite after another, as they were called for. At length Elinor turned and looked about the room.

Little by little, the groups scattered around the parlor had drawn nearer the piano. All of them were watching her, eager for her to sing again, while her eyes moved up and down the room, enjoying her first little triumph. Wyckoff was murmuring half-mocking compliments in her ear; but she turned away from him, and unconsciously her eyes sought his cousin, to see if he were aware of her success. At first she looked for him in vain; but at length she saw him sitting quite alone at the far end of the room, with his head resting on his hand, which shaded his face. Then her conscience smote her, for, angry at his tone the night before, she had purposely avoided him, all that day. It was plain that he was unhappy now, whether or not from her studied neglect, she could not tell.

" Please sing just once more, Miss Tiemann," Wyckoff was urging her. " Sing alone now, just this once."

"Her voice is glorious," an old lady from Boston was saying behind her fan; "and her method is going to be perfect. I can't tell what it is; and yet, after all, her singing is unsatisfactory. Down underneath it all, there's a little coldness, as if she never quite read the composer's real thought."

Elinor stood hesitating for a moment, still with her eyes fixed upon the lonely figure far across the room. She had never been more beautiful than she was then, in her simple white gown, and with the brilliant flush on her cheeks, the dark glow of excitement in her eyes. All at once she turned to the piano, and, with a whispered word to Miss Whitney, took her place and began the accompaniment to the little old "Schlummerlied" she had sung at Idlewilde, three years before.

No coldness was in her voice now. She was singing for one hearer alone, and half unconsciously asking for his pardon. There was a little unsteady note in her voice at the close; then came a hush, followed by a quick murmur of applause.

Refusing all their entreaties to sing again, she rose and crossed the room to Heaton's side.

"I have sung till I am tired," she said. "Won't you please take me out on the piazza for a little air?"

And they went away together.

CHAPTER FOURTEEN

ONE morning, less than a week after her return to the city, Elinor was walking up Fifth Avenue. She had been down town for her first lesson of the season, and Arturo had warmly welcomed her back to his studio. She had lingered a little after her lesson, to talk over her plans for the coming winter. Then, tempted by the clear, breezy morning, she had resolved to walk up town again, while she thought over at her leisure the recent conversation.

It had needed little consideration to decide Elinor to return to New York for at least one more year with Signor Arturo. Her year's training had done so much for her that her friends were unanimous in their advice to her to go on with her study; and she was more than ready to be influenced by their opinion. She had worked with a will, and, notwithstanding Arturo's lectures, he was not a little proud of his pupil. And Elinor, in spite of her frequent discouragements, felt that she was slowly working towards the realization of her dreams.

They might never come true; but, as time went on, her hopes were not limited so entirely to the public appearance which should be the grand climax of her career. She was slowly learning to love her work for its own sake, not for the personal triumph which it might one day bring her. It was as Heaton had predicted: the more she gained this unselfish interest in her voice and her art, the nearer she was coming to the fulfilment of her former hopes, and day after day the prospect was brightening before her.

She had not seen the Emersons since the night of their return. The past few days had been busy ones for her, and she knew that Mrs. Emerson would be occupied in setting the wheels of her domestic machinery once more in motion. Now she resolved to see her before the day was over. There were many things to be talked over together. After a month of daily intercourse, it is hard to drop back all at once into the occasional meetings of ordinary friendship.

If Elinor had but known it, the last thought included Mrs. Emerson's brother much more than it did Mrs. Emerson herself. Far more than she had realized it at the time, she had enjoyed her close companionship with Heaton, and she found that she missed him to a most unreasonable extent. Day after day throughout that long month, he had been at hand whenever she wanted him, always interested and sympathetic, whatever her mood might be, and never obtruding himself at the wrong time. It was given to few women, she thought to herself, to have such a friend. A year ago, even, she would have said it belonged to the class of impossible situations evolved by the novelist. It was a great gift, this frank, unreserved friendship of a broad-minded man, and she was glad that fate had thrown it in her way. The thought had never once crossed her mind that, to the man himself, this friendship might have quite another signification. Heaton's self-control, during those trying days at the lake, had been all that he had desired; in the girl's eyes they were friends, simply friends and nothing more.

She had crossed over to Fifth Avenue, and was strolling up the shady side of the street, opposite the wall of the reservoir. So absorbed was she in her reverie that she had not noticed the carriage which drew up at the curbstone, and she started violently when Mrs. Emerson's voice fell upon her ears.

"Elinor! And is it thus that you disdain us?"

Laughing and blushing at her own absent-mindedness, the girl came forward to the carriage.

"Bertha, how you startled me! I was just pondering upon a question of vast importance: whether, if I called on you, this afternoon, you would ask me to stay to dinner. I've the accumulated events of a week to talk over with your brother," she added gayly, as she leaned across Mrs. Emerson to take Heaton's outstretched hand.

"We'll put an extra bone in the soup, and hang out the latchstring," he answered, with one of his rare sunny smiles. He looked tired, that morning, and his eyes had dark shadows underneath them, like the eyes of a man who had been passing through some great nervous strain. However, there was no mistaking the pleasure he felt at their meeting, and Elinor felt an answering thrill of pleasure as she watched him.

"Get in and let us take you home," Mrs. Emerson suggested hospitably. "We are going within a block of your house, so it will be no trouble. I've an engagement, this noon, or I should insist upon your going back to lunch with us now. I had to bring my little brother home from his kindergarten," she went on, as Elinor stepped into the carriage and, with a quick motion, anticipated Heaton, who was rising to give her his seat at Mrs. Emerson's side.

"Don't move," she said hastily. "Truly, I like this place better; I can talk to you both at the same time if I sit facing you, and that is always an object to me, you know. But what about the kindergarten? Is it a joke?"

The life died out of Heaton's face. He looked suddenly older and graver and less strong, as he answered, —

"It's not in the least a joke, Miss Tiemann. I'm trying to make the best of things, as you suggested, last June. I have left my lofty solitude, and joined the ranks of the professional blind. In other words, I have gone into the school for the blind, over here, and have set to work to study Braille, side by side with the babes of the institution. In time it may be a benefit to me; but the process is rather painful."

He threw out the last words defiantly; then he sat silent, with his teeth shut hard upon his lower lip, which, after all, was not quite steady. The past two hours had been an unexpectedly bitter experience for him. It had been hard for the sensitive, self-contained man to leave his sheltered surroundings and feel himself one of a vast class of afflicted humanity for whom institutions had been mercifully provided. His nerves were quivering, and he felt his self-control fast giving way. And yet, strange to say, it was a relief to speak of it to Elinor. He had an instinctive feeling that she would understand.

At his unexpected change of tone, the girl experienced a slight shock. For an instant, she hesitated and glanced appealingly at his sister who did not meet her eyes, but sat with her own fixed on the old gray wall of the reservoir. Between friends, the most eloquent expression of sympathy is often given without a spoken word, but Elinor suddenly realized that in that way she was powerless to reach the man before her. Never before had the barrier of his blindness seemed to rise up so impenetrably between them.

"I was afraid it would be hard for you," she said at last, and her voice was very gentle and pitiful; "but I had no idea what it really must be. I can see now, and I wish I had never spoken of it."

"It's better that you did," he answered, while his fingers closed nervously on the knob of her parasol beside him. "It will be a good thing for me, when once I learn their writing, for then I can correct my own work and save Bertha all but the copy. It will be a relief to be more independent, and to be able to go back over my work and see what I am doing. But this is only my first day, you know—" He paused abruptly.

"And the work is harder than you thought it would be?" Elinor asked, as again she tried to catch Mrs. Emerson's eye. From the first, she had found it hard to meet the glance of his sister, whenever Heaton was speaking of himself. It was as if Mrs. Emerson felt that there was a certain disloyalty in thus taking advantage of his blindness.

"It's not the work," he said, with an accent of utter dreariness which Elinor had never heard from him before. "I can work as well as any of them; but I've been alone too long. Living, as I do, in the midst of people who can see and who have some notion of what tact means, I regard my case as being unique and myself as being almost as good as any of you. And then to be suddenly dropped into a roomful of just such people, to know that, to all eternity, you can't see them. nor they you, that you can't have any notion of each other except by the voice, or when they accidentally joggle against you — " He paused, with a sudden catch in his breath. His face was white and his lips were dry and rigid. Then his grasp on the knob beside him grew tighter, while he went on slowly; "I think I am beginning to see what it all means. Not to myself; God knows I found that out, several months ago; but to you all. I had never realized till to-day how I must seem to you, and how apart from you my life must be."

The next moment, he felt Elinor's little gloved hand rest on his, where it clutched the porcelain ball.

"Mr. Heaton," she said steadily; "if your life is apart from ours, it is only because the grandness of your courage has put you on a plane we can never reach. We can't know what it is to be blind and to drop out of active life, as you have done; but at least we can know what it is to have met an unselfish, heroic man, and, for my part, I thank you for the lesson."

Fearful of having said too much, she broke off, and for the next three or four blocks, no word was spoken. It was Heaton who finally broke the silence. In quite his usual tone, he asked about Arturo and the morning's lesson, and they were still talking about matters musical when the carriage stopped at Elinor's door.

Late the same afternoon, Heaton and Elinor were left alone for a few moments in the Emersons' library. All at once, Heaton recurred to the subject of the morning's talk.

" I'm not always such a coward," he said briefly; " but the hurt was fresh at the time, and I wanted to make a public demand upon your sympathy. I'm sorry to have made a scene; but the conditions were new, and I had n't adjusted myself to them yet. There are days when I feel as if the darkness must break for just an hour or two, to let me catch my breath and pull my courage together once more. I shall get my mental balance again before long. Till then, you must either cut my acquaintance, or be patient with me."

As he spoke, he drew his hand across his face, while his mouth, under his little brown mustache, worked nervously. He was silent for a moment; then he broke out again, —

" Really, Miss Tiemann, I'm not as much of a coward as I seem. You don't know what it is. Nobody does, who has never been blind. When the oculist told me I was going blind, I supposed I understood what he meant, that it was going to be a species of perpetual night. It isn't that at all. I used to lie awake, nights, and think about it, and watch the grayish outlines of the windows, and I fancied I knew all about it. Then, one day, without any warning at all, I found that I knew absolutely nothing. It presses in on me so, and chokes me, and weighs me down. And then the hardest thing of all has been to get used to the endlessness of it. Even now there are times when I feel as if it couldn't last, and I begin to plan what I will do when I can see again. But that doesn't stay long, and the blackness settles down tight around me till I can hardly breathe, and I feel as if I must either shriek, or go mad. Do you wonder I'm half afraid, and want to hold on to somebody? It isn't enough to hear; I must touch people, to make sure I'm not all alone in the dark."

He had been pacing the floor restlessly; but now he came forward to the fire and groped about for his usual seat, which had been pushed away to the farther side of the room. Elinor felt that she could bear no more. All his proud self-control and courage appeared to have broken down, and it was as if, for the hour, he were making an open avowal of his weakness. As he stood there in the gathering dusk and shut within his own greater darkness, her thoughts flashed back to that other Heaton she had known in the old days. Only three years had passed; but now it was all so changed.

Rising, she crossed the room and brought his chair forward to the fire.

"Here it is," she said. "It was moved away."

He stretched out his hand, touched it, and slowly seated himself. There was no gratitude in his face, nothing but infinite sadness, as he asked, —

"Miss Tiemann, do you ever remember Idlewilde?"

"Don't," she said brokenly. "Perhaps it will be easier in time."

CHAPTER FIFTEEN

"I HAD a perfect orgy with Arturo, to-day," Elinor said, as she bent over the fire to pick up a burning brand fallen on the tiles.

Heaton laughed.

"The old story. What was it, this time? Or was it sacred to the deities of music, and not to be repeated to profane ears?"

"It was profane, if that's what you mean," she retorted. "I can't imagine how a man who knows so little English has ever contrived to gain such perfect command of our expletives. His praise is slow and halting; but he swears fluently. This time, I brought it upon myself. I had ventured to apply for admission to the Oratorio Society without asking his consent."

"The Oratorio Society?" said Mrs. Emerson. "Jack is in it again, this year; isn't he, Tom?"

"He is one of the shining lights among their tenors," her brother responded.

Elinor looked slightly annoyed.

"I didn't know that," she said.

"Yes, he has sung there for years, and he talks as if the fate of the whole musical world were hanging upon the performances of that

149

one organization. Every year, he threatens to get out of it, and every year finds him firm at his post. But what was Arturo's objection to your going into it?"

" 'Because it will serve to make your voice so very promiscuous,' " returned Elinor, dropping into her teacher's voice and manner. "I can't find that it is likely to do me any other harm. I have been so anxious to study one of the great oratorios, and as long as I am not likely to be asked to pose as soloist, my solitary chance lies in turning promiscuous and joining the ranks. I have only rehearsed with them once; but it was much finer than I had supposed."

"And did you feel properly promiscuous?" Heaton asked teasingly.

"I most certainly did. They have put me on the end of the sopranos, and that leaves me sandwiched in between an Irish lady in a pink silk waist, and a lean little tenor who can't go above *F sharp*. He stops and coughs behind his hand, every time the others soar above him. I suppose it is intended as an apology to me for his flatting; but he might allow once telling me to answer for every time. There's not a single person in sight whom I ever saw before, and I am forlorn as can be during the intermission; but when the music starts up again, I am content."

"I will tell Jack to hunt you up," Mrs. Emerson said. "What about the Saturday Club? You know you promised to sing for us, this fall."

"If you dare trust me," she replied, laughing. "I am getting to doubt my ability to do anything but chirp a little. Arturo does n't increase one's courage, and I may break down, at the last moment."

"Arturo is a beast," Heaton observed.

"No; he 's not," Elinor answered quickly. "I am giving you an absolutely wrong impression of him. He is glorious, simply glorious; and it is an inspiration to work with such a man. Even if I never amount to anything, I shall always be glad I came to him, for he makes music so much broader and deeper than other men. I used to suppose it was something to play with; now I believe it is something to live for."

Heaton's face lighted.

"You 'll get there, Miss Tiemann, if you keep on. It 's the working for something, after all, that counts for more than the something attained."

But Elinor had digressed again. It was characteristic of her to speak seriously for only a moment at a time, and then to drop back into a lighter mood.

"He is a tyrant, though," she remarked thoughtfully; "a tyrant of the worst kind. I have learned to obey him in all things, to avoid Huyler, and overshoes, and light songs, to keep my tongue under strict control, and to sound my final consonants; but, alas! I haven't learned not to sing off the key occasionally, when my feelings are too many for me. He says it is a crying shame, and, do you know, he hasn't the least suspicion that therein lurks a pun. He worships key, anyway. I believe he keeps one hanging in his room, to pray to, o' nights; and his whole future happiness would be lost to him, if his golden harp should happen to be a little flat on one of the strings. Your absolutely accurate people are always a trifle disagreeable, anyway."

"What a heretic you are!" Heaton said, laughing at her sudden outburst.

There was something whimsical about her conversation which suited his mood. She had a fashion of talking on the surface of things, with an undercurrent of deeper meaning, now lending an air of mock solemnity to matters of trivial import, now talking the random nonsense of a little child. Then, of a sudden, she dropped all these freaks and spoke with the sincerity of an earnest woman. From the first of their acquaintance, Heaton had enjoyed her conversation, and had delighted in drawing her on to a free expression of her opinions, which were always original and always daring.

"I'm not heretical," she said defensively. "But once in a while I feel as if I were hemmed in by rules and regulations, and then I rebel. I want to sing De Koven, and to flat, too, if I feel like it. It is hard to live up to yourself, every day, just as it would be hard to stand on tiptoe forever. Now and then, I want to drop back to the firmer foothold of my natural depravity. When I do drop back, I hate it; but it is just as attractive to look down upon. I wonder if self-made people don't want to go back to their original level sometimes."

"I think I don't like self-made people," Heaton remarked reflectively.

"Why not? I think they are magnificent," she flashed hotly. "That is the old chasm between the West and the East, and we shall never agree."

"I admire them, too, theoretically," he returned; "but, for practical acquaintance, I prefer the born-so type. The new ones are always in too much of a hurry to get themselves into shape before they die. They can't spend time, poor things, to get all their corners rubbed down; while the others have been being polished for ever and ever so many generations. You will feel it, even in singing. Other things being equal, here in America you will find that an Alden or an Endicott will sing better than an O'Flarity."

"I'm not so sure of it," she answered thoughtfully. "But you can test your theory, if I sing for the Saturday Club. I believe Miss Roach is to sing, too, and she certainly is virgin soil, so far as her ancestors are concerned. Arturo claims to have discovered her when she was selling flowers on one of the ferries."

Already their life at the lake had faded from a present interest to a past memory, and they were settling down to their regular occupations of the winter. To Heaton it seemed strange to be in harness again. Both at home and at the school, he was working hard at his Braille, and the pain he had felt at the start was slowly yielding to his pleasure in once more mastering a difficult task. It had been real enough at first, the shock of mingling with those other blind people from whom he was so isolated, and there were hours when the sense of their nearness made him long to rush away from them and forget them. Their ways annoyed him strangely. It seemed as if they were trying to impress upon him that he was just like all the rest of them, one of a class to be rated with drunken men and paupers in the census reports. He established relations with none of them, but went his way, reserved and alone. Since his one outburst, on that first day, he had said little of his work; but he had toiled at it unceasingly, bringing to it all the vigor of a well-disciplined mind, until little by little he gained skill in this new study which was destined one day to be so useful to him.

He had never understood his outbreak to Elinor, that day. Neither did he altogether regret it. He had borne his fate in silence for so long that there was a certain relief in this sudden outcry for pity. If she had met him in any other way, the memory would have been galling to him now; but her sympathy had been quick and generous, and it had left no scar upon his self-respect. In the supreme moment of his suffering, he had called upon her womanhood for help, and it had answered to his call.

Since they had returned to the city, Elinor had been a much less frequent guest at the Emersons'. It was not that she was less intimate with them; but, spurred on by a rare word of approval from Arturo, she was practising more diligently than ever. To-day, however, dropping in for a cup of tea, she had found Mrs. Emerson and her brother sitting alone by the library fire.

"Our friends have all deserted us, to-day," Mrs. Emerson said, as she took forcible possession of Elinor's jacket; "and you are surely going to stay here to dine with us. Jack is coming, too, and we shall be as cosy as can be.

You must stay to wake us up, for we are deplorably dull, now that Ned has gone back to school again."

Heaton had been in one of his old gay moods. They came more rarely than ever, since his return to the city; but, on this particular afternoon, he had been in unwonted spirits. Wyckoff, when he appeared at dinner time, found them in a state of wild hilarity.

"Miss Tiemann and Tom have been talking over old times," Mrs. Emerson explained, as she rose to meet her cousin. "I have been absolutely appalled at their confessions. Tom admits to countless sins, and even Miss Tiemann is trying to make him remember her saying 'By Jiminy,' one night, when she tumbled out of a wagon."

"Don't think it is my usual form of speech, Mr. Wyckoff," Elinor interposed, as he seated himself at her side. "I caught it from a naughty little cousin, and I only use it under stress of circumstances, — such as going for the doctor in the dead of night," she added, with a merry sidelong glance at Heaton.

It was always hard for her to realize that he was shut out from such byplay as this, and she never failed to receive a little shock, when she met his quiet, unresponsive gaze.

"I shall always feel defrauded over losing that week," Wyckoff answered. "I 've an idea that Tom was far-seeing when he proposed my going away."

" It was a good thing you did," Elinor replied audaciously, " You would have been entirely too worldly a figure, and you never would have harmonized with your environment. Mr. Heaton and I were as innocently rustic as a pair of babes in the wood, and even my decorous little aunt unbends, when she is in the wilderness; but I am convinced that you could never have been one of us, in spite of Mr. Kurzenbeine's good opinion of you."

" Kurzenbeine? I'd forgotten him."

" Another proof of what I was saying. I saw him, last summer, and he was still chanting your praises."

" I remember him now; he was that tall, yellow-headed German of a literal turn of mind. I told him, one night, that my ancestors were all Russian Jews. He believed me implicitly, in spite of Tom's attempts to re-establish his belief in the respectable roots of our family tree."

Since they had come back to the city, Wyckoff had not allowed his friendship with Elinor to die out. From time to time, he had met her at the Emersons', and he had called upon her frequently. By this time there had grown up between them a free-and-easy good-fellowship; and now, as they left the dinner table, he had followed Elinor back to the library, where they had fallen into a long discussion of Arturo, the Oratorio Society, and the dozen and one interests which they had in common.

Heaton sat by in silence. Envious as he might be of their common interests from which he was excluded, there was never any bitterness in his mind, so far as his cousin was concerned. In the time of his greatest need it had been Jack who had come to his aid and helped him through one of the hardest experiences of his life. If someone else must come in between himself and Elinor and monopolize her for an hour, he could most willingly give place to his cousin. Jack had earned the right to his good times. However, it gave him a sense of isolation to sit and listen to their talk of people and places of which he was ignorant.

At length Elinor looked up and saw him. He was sitting alone at the other side of the broad hearth, moodily twisting his mustache and frowning at the fire. . Already he was beginning to show the effects of the strain under which he had been living for the past three or four months. He was thinner than of old; new lines had come into his face, and his hair had grown gray about the temples; but his expression had become more strong and manly, and the quiet dignity which she had known at Idlewilde, the dignity of ripening manhood, had changed into that greater dignity of sorrow borne in courageous silence.

"There are times," Wyckoff said to Mrs. Emerson, one day, with the sudden light in his blue eyes which came only when he was deeply moved; "there are times when I feel like taking off my hat before Tom. He doesn't live like the rest of us, somehow, and we can only stand and watch him, and keep still."

With some trivial excuse, Elinor rose, leaving Wyckoff alone, and crossed to Heaton's side.

"I have just been reading over the story you wrote, last summer," she said, as she took the chair at his side; "the one you let me read when we were at the lake, you know. What ever put it into your head?"

"Why?" he asked, turning slowly to face her.

"It is so different from the others, so full of fun and ridiculous situations. I kept wishing, while I was reading it, that I could have looked in on you when you wrote it. You must have had ever so much fun out of it, all alone by yourself."

Heaton's face had grown very white.

"I don't remember enjoying myself so very much, when I wrote it," he said dryly. "I am afraid you will have to excuse me, Miss Tiemann. I promised Edwin I would be in the smoking-room, to-night. Charlie Bennett was coming over, for an hour." And he rose and went away out of the room.

CHAPTER SIXTEEN

WHAT a blessing it is that our minds are not self-registering machines, like a phonograph! There is not one of us who would not be rather appalled, if suddenly confronted with a full and exact transcription of his thoughts, during any given period. Fortunate it is for us that, although the imprint of our thoughts is left upon us, yet our mortal eyes can only see the page as a whole, without being able to make out the separate type.

The last two or three months had marked the beginning of a new era in Heaton's life. Up to this time, he had entered closely into the home life about him. His writing had taken but a small part of his time, and he had spent his leisure moments with his sister. Now, although of late he had lost interest in his work, he preferred to pass most of his hours in his own room.

There was little variety in his employment there, only the going over and over again the question of his love for Elinor, now making all sorts of excuses to justify himself in telling her the whole story and begging her to be his wife, if only for the sake of the luxurious life he could afford to give her; now planning how he could secretly work to win her love, to enter into her life and interests so closely that she would some day waken to the knowledge that, without him at her side, her own life would be incomplete; then spurning the whole, as unworthy of his manhood, only to begin again, the next moment, and go on hoping and planning and dreaming, until he was called away and forced into an active interest outside of himself.

Again and again he resolved to be a man, to forget all but his pleasant friendship with Elinor and to enjoy that, without a thought of anything beyond. The next day, the old questions would come uppermost, and the *If—If—Ifs* would rush through his brain in never-ending circles. If he had been a man in active life, he would have been despicable; but now, shut in and limited as he was, he was more to be pitied. He despised himself most acutely at times, however. It was so beneath all his ideals of what a man should feel and think. He only gained a partial respect for himself when he remembered that, in spite of all his temptations, he had never yet betrayed his love. He hoped that the secret might always remain his own; but he was proving so much weaker than he had supposed himself to be, that he felt it was impossible to trust himself beyond the present hour.

Between his days of moody dreaming and his hours of careful self-restraint when he was with Elinor, his temper began to suffer. He was no longer as quiet and even as before; but often his overstrained nerves sought relief in cold disregard, or in an occasional cutting word. It left her surprised and hurt, though she showed a quick generosity in her forgiveness. Worst of all, he himself realized that he was losing his mental perspective, that he took himself too much in earnest, and magnified trifles until they assumed colossal proportions. It would have been a relief if he could have seen the ridiculous side of the situation. He vaguely felt that it was there; but he was unable to grasp it.

It had been arranged that Elinor was to sing before the Saturday Club, that season, and the promised event came off, one night in November. The members of the club had been allowed to invite freely for the musicale, and the Emersons' large house was filled to overflowing. To Elinor, sitting up-stairs and listening to the hum of voices below, it promised to be something of an ordeal. By a tacit consent, she had been recognized as the star of the evening, and this was her first introduction to a New York audience. Strange to say, Arturo had favored her singing, and, for several lessons, he had been training her carefully upon the work he had chosen for her.

"We shall see what you can do, signorina," he said, one day. "I have hopes of you, great hopes, for you have the voice and you shall have the method. That I shall give you. But you must enter into the work *con amore, con amore* which means with love. As yet you do not seem to have the soul under beneath your singing which shall make all right. You can sing now to be applauded; but you must sing to make the tears fall in a storm. A singer must feel it here, in the heart, signorina; she is never made from the head. Now when you begin to sing this aria, you must believe that you are in heaven, and all the people around you are angels."

Elinor herself felt that this was her first great opportunity, and she longed to succeed, if only to justify Arturo in the encouragement he had given her. But as she sat there alone, listening to the murmur from below, realizing that all those strange people were there to hear her and to pass judgment upon her, her courage suddenly failed. Many of her audience had heard the world's best singers. What right had she to come before them? She rose and began to pace the room hastily.

Heaton's den had been set aside for her use, that night. It was the first time she had been there, and she found a partial distraction for her thoughts in looking about her. The room had been fitted up for him, long ago, and for years it had remained unchanged. The mantel was covered with a collection of photographs of women in the dress of four or five years before. Among them, she recognized many of the women whom she had met at the Emersons', women who now rarely spoke to the man whom once they had known so well. In one corner was a group of sketches of Idlewilde, arranged about a central drawing of herself. She gave a little smile of gratified vanity, as she saw, from the initials in the corners of the sketches, that they were the work of Wyckoff. She remembered the gown so well; it was the one she had worn, the day she and Heaton had first met.

Across the room was the orderly writing-table, and beside it, on a little stand, was a pile of books. She took them up to glance at their titles. Most of them bore the imprint of the year of his blindness; but, half-way down the pile, she came upon one that called forth a little exclamation of surprise. It was a shabby paper-covered novel, with her name written across the outside. At a loss to recognize it and to account for its being there, she picked it up and opened it. On the flyleaf were a few lines, written carelessly in pencil, rubbed and blurred with time. She knew the writing by instinct, although she had rarely seen it before.

"On the window pelted the raindrops,
  The storm was raging outside;
Into the cottage for shelter
  From our path we turned us aside.
And there, by the homely window,
  Sat an aged, wrinkled dame,
While above the hum of her spindle
  We heard her dull refrain,—
''S ist Alles zu kurz, zu kurz!'

"Out into the burning sunshine
  We took our careless way;
Naught heeded we of her murmur,
  Life was so fair, that day.
But now that the dream has faded
  And the hours have flown away,
Swinging alone in my hammock,
  I echo the old dame's lay,
''S ist Alles zu kurz, zu kurz!'"

A step was heard outside, and Heaton's voice
asked, —

"May I come in?"

She whirled around suddenly. Her face had
lighted, and her eyes were shining with pleasure.

"Did you really write this, Mr. Heaton?" she
asked, holding up the book.

"What do you mean?" he said, as he crossed
the room to her side. On the way, he collided
with a chair which she had pushed from its
usual place; but, for the moment, she was too
eager to heed it.

"''S ist Alles zu kurz,'" she quoted. "And

you told me once that you had never written a line of poetry."

It seemed to Heaton that his secret had been shouted from the housetops. He had quite forgotten the crude lines, hastily written so long ago; but, word for word, they came back to him now with startling distinctness. What would she think of him? He felt a sudden resentment towards the girl, who had ventured to pry into his papers, to ferret out the secrets of his private life. He turned upon her one look of scorn. It was his only way to recover his lost ground, to bury again what she had brought to light.

"It could hardly be called poetry," he said coldly. "It's only the merest doggerel. Besides, I really can't see how you chanced to find it."

His accent was cutting, and the quick tears sprang into Elinor's eyes. His rebuke had touched her keenly, but she was too proud to seek to justify herself. She turned and silently put the book into his hand.

"Forgive me," she said, after a pause. "I had no idea of finding it here."

Impatiently he tossed the book down on the writing-table.

"It's of no consequence, anyway," he said indifferently. "You are welcome to it, if you wish."

"Elinor, dear," Mrs. Emerson said from the

doorway; "the next number is yours, so perhaps you 'd better come down."

Forcing back her tears, the girl slowly turned away and crossed the room.

"I 'll do my best, Bertha," she said drearily. " I am afraid I sha' n't succeed well in my début; but you must be merciful."

A moment later, she came forward on the little stage which had been built out at the side of the room. Her face was white and still, and, of a sudden, dark lines had settled about her eyes. She looked tired and discouraged, not at all like her usual bright, careless self.

During the short introduction, she glanced about the room. It was crowded with people, many of them strangers; but she could not seem to separate the faces. Here and there she caught the flash of diamonds, or the shimmer of some gown of unusually vivid color; otherwise the crowd before her was like a uniform mass of humanity. Down in the foreground, she recognized Arturo, staring intently at her and beaming encouragement from every line of his round face; and, far back in a corner of the room, she saw Heaton, who had just come in with his cousin. His face was stern and troubled; and, do what she would, she could not turn her eyes from it, though she felt the lump rising in her throat again and swelling until the pain of it choked her.

The prelude was ended, and she began to sing. She was surprised at the steadiness of her voice. It was clear and firm, but so remote and monotonous. It seemed to her to have no connection with herself; it was as if she were singing from the acquired momentum of her past training, and her present will had nothing to do with it. She realized that she was singing coldly, mechanically; but she was powerless, for the time being, to throw herself into the spirit of the composer. She could only repeat to herself, —

"It's of no consequence, anyway. It's of no consequence, anyway."

She made one strong effort, as she reached the closing phrase; but though she took her high note perfectly, and sustained it with an ease for which she had never dared to hope, she left the stage amidst the coldest, most perfunctory applause.

Alas for the encore for which Arturo had made such careful preparation! Her possible triumph had proved to be an actual failure. She caught one glimpse of Arturo's disappointed face, and without waiting for him to come to her, she had turned away and wearily mounted the stairs again.

Wyckoff and Mrs. Emerson joined her there almost immediately. Her lashes were wet; but she had regained something of her usual manner, and she laughed nervously, as she met them.

"Scold me, if you like, Bertha," she said. "I meant well; but I was powerless to carry out my good intentions. I am sorry to have disgraced you; but I have an idea that it is harder for me than for you."

Mrs. Emerson was silent. She had overheard her brother's words to Elinor, a quarter of an hour before, and her womanly intuition told her the secret of the girl's absolute failure. But Wyckoff tried to find something to say.

Elinor turned to him proudly.

"Don't try to console me, Mr. Wyckoff. We all know that I sang detestably, so what is the use of denying the fact? Some time or other, I will sing so that you can congratulate me. Till then, the less said, the better."

Late that evening, after the guests had gone away, Mrs. Emerson came into the library where Heaton still sat over the dying fire.

"Tom," she said gently; "were n't you a little hard on Elinor, to-night?"

He raised his head impatiently.

"How do you mean?" he asked.

"When you were in your room," she answered. "I happened to hear it, and I thought you were too severe. I don't know what to make of you lately, Tom; you are so changeable with Elinor. It is too bad for you to play with her as you do."

"Play with her? How do I play with her?" he asked, forcing his voice to be so quiet that it was devoid of all expression.

"You treat her so differently at different times," his sister went on, little dreaming of the pain she was causing her hearer, who sat silent, with his face shielded from the heat of the fire and from her searching eyes. "One day, you are friendly to her; the next, you are so cold. Elinor is very fond of you, Tom. She has been here so much that you must seem almost like a brother to her, and it is too bad for you to hurt her in this way."

"I am sorry," he said slowly. "I did n't know I did. I won't, any more."

But after his sister had left him alone, he rose and stood motionless for a long time, with his arm resting against the mantel, his head on his arm.

At length he broke the silence.

"Oh, God, have pity!" he moaned.

CHAPTER SEVENTEEN

"Isn't this the ideal of luxury?" Elinor exclaimed gayly, as she came into the dining-room, the next morning.

She looked a little tired and her eyes were heavy, otherwise there was nothing to show that she had lain awake, half the night, over her failure of the previous evening. It had been a severe blow to her, after all her bright anticipations of success; but she was at no loss to account for it, and she felt that it in no way concerned her real ability. The slightest circumstance had changed the whole result of the evening, and had brought disaster and disappointment upon herself. She could only look forward to the future and hope that sometime she would be asked to sing again, when she could redeem her reputation. Meanwhile, she was too human not to feel a deep resentment towards Heaton. His rudeness to her had been inexcusable. He alone had been the cause of her inability to throw herself into the music, and sing as she had so often dreamed of singing.

Over and over again she asked herself why he was so changeable in his manner to her.

She could see no cause for his occasional harshness; it was rude and ungentlemanly and altogether unlike himself. Wyckoff could never have been guilty·of such discourtesy; but then, neither could his cousin, four years ago. That was it. She must lay it all to his trouble, to the disappointment in all his plans, and be as generous as she could be to forgive. She would have felt justified in cutting the acquaintance of another man upon less provocation; but with Heaton it was all so different.

It had been agreed that she should not go back to the boarding-house until the following Monday. After she was in her room, that night, Mrs. Emerson had gone to her, and she had stayed for a long hour, talking over the evening's events. Although neither of the women had touched upon the real cause of Elinor's disaster, Mrs. Emerson had left her feeling in some measure comforted. At least, it was a relief to find that her friends still believed in her talent. It gave her new courage to go on. Failure was inevitable at times; it was not necessarily final.

As she met Heaton, the next morning, she was struck anew by the signs of age and sadness in his face. He showed that he, too, had passed a sleepless night, and he greeted her with a little manner of hesitation which asked for pardon more eloquently than words could have done.

"What is it?" he inquired now, as he seated himself. "You are a true optimist, Miss Tiemann, and everything is rose-color to you."

"So much the better," she answered. "Rose-color is becoming to most people, and I like optimists. I feel like one, to-day. After my experience, last night, it is good to be allowed to spend the day here, just as if I had n't disgraced you all. Moreover, I have worked hard enough, this last week, to make me appreciate the delights of settling down here for a lazy, rainy Sunday, with no one likely to interrupt us."

"It had n't occurred to me to be thankful for this rain," observed Mr. Emerson; "but I suppose I must rejoice on your account."

"Certainly," she responded promptly. "The sight of you, starting off to church with mackintosh and umbrella, will only serve to enhance my appreciation of my own comfort. Even the honor of being senior warden of a popular church has its inherent disadvantages. Nothing is perfect without a little contrast; is it, Mr. Heaton? To make my bliss complete, I had a new novel sent me, yesterday, and I was inspired to bring it with me. As soon as we get rid of your husband, Bertha, the rest of us will curl up by the library fire and give ourselves over to that most delicious of combinations, a new book and a rainy day."

An hour later, she came down the stairs, book in hand. She had exchanged her close-fitting gown for a waist of bright, soft silk. It was a bewildering combination of frills and puffs, yet it seemed to suit her rounded, girlish figure, and the vivid bit of color was a relief from the dull background of a stormy November day. Heaton and his sister had settled themselves beside the fire, which was snapping and crackling with a cosy sound of comfort. Elinor curled herself up in a corner of the broad couch in the midst of a nest of many-colored cushions, with her back to the window and her head turned so that she could watch Heaton over the top of her book. She had learned that his face was prompt to show his enjoyment, and she liked to follow the course of her story, written in his changing expressions.

For two hours she read steadily, while the fire crackled and the rain swept against the windows. Now and then she paused, as she turned a leaf or began a new chapter, to make some comment upon the story. Mrs. Emerson was absorbed in the book; but Heaton, underneath his appreciation of the plot and its skilful development, was giving himself up wholly to the enjoyment of their quiet, homelike morning together.

It was a long time since they had spent a day like this. Usually there was something to break in upon their good time, some one to monopolize

Elinor and keep her talking of interests in which he had no part. This was like the earlier days of their friendship, and it followed the excitement of the night before, as the chorale follows the fugue. For the hour, it was good to stop living and merely to exist. For one moment, it occurred to him how pleasant it would be to spend his life in this way, to have her always near him, willing to read the latest books to him and to talk them over, in the domestic atmosphere of their own fireside. Then he put the thought away from him impatiently. The present was all that could be desired; the future must take care of itself.

Later in the morning, when Mrs. Emerson was called away for a few moments, Elinor dropped the book, face downward, in her lap, and leaned back among her cushions.

"I wonder if it is on account of my knowing you and your stories," she said musingly; "that now I never read a novel without wondering how the author felt and what he really meant, when he wrote this or that."

"I suppose books are always something of a patchwork of one's own observations and experiences," Heaton remarked. "Mercifully for us, though, most people don't read them, microscope in hand, hunting for the seams."

"I never used to do it," she answered; "but lately I find myself trying to read between the lines. Most of all, I wonder what sort of a person the author has in mind, when he makes his hero or heroine. I know there must always be somebody in the background, even if he does n't admit it to himself."

"Fancy depicting the adventures of a pure abstraction!" Heaton laughed. "I 'm afraid the result would n't be very human or very sympathetic. I confess that I used to start with the skeleton of some one I had met, and then pad it out to suit myself. Lately I have rather left that off, though. Women are my trials. My men I can work up from myself; but I have to carry most women through a story on the strength of gray eyes, or a dimple in one cheek."

"I might keep a notebook for your use," she suggested laughingly, while she twisted the little bracelet on her left wrist.

"I am in earnest about it," he replied. "I find that lately, as my memory grows less reliable, I have to do most of my descriptive work at random. It hampers me badly, and I don't want it to show in my writing."

"I had n't thought of it before," Elinor said gently. "Your stories don't show it yet; but, if there ever should be any danger of it, could n't Bertha help you, or I?"

"Thank you for thinking to offer, anyway. Did I tell you that I am really getting to be fairly proficient in Braille? It's a great help to me already, for now I can read over my work and have some idea of what I am doing. But please don't think that I bore everybody with my work as I do you, Miss Tiemann. There is something about you that makes me egotistic, I'm afraid."

"It is probably contagious," she answered merrily. "You ought to know by this time how interested I am in it, and in the greater success which you are going to have, some day. Only don't forget all your old friends, when you are sitting calmly perched on the topmost pinnacle of fame." And she took up her book again, as Mrs. Emerson came back into the room.

How many people to whom we readily confide our plans and hopes and aspirations are like the *pot-pourri* jar in which the young society man has been said to stow away the roses given him by different maidens! In either case, the offering is willingly received, sometimes begged or demanded; but once taken in, it quickly loses all individuality of being or association. Some people are born to receive confidences. Their sympathy and interest may be genuine while they last; but they speedily die away, leaving no permanent trace behind them.

"Miss Tiemann gets up a great reputation for her intelligence," remarked the worldly-wise

Ned, one day. "It's funny that you fellows don't get on to it. She pumps each one of you about your pet hobby; then she passes on the information to the next man, and astonishes him with knowing so much in so many lines. She's a schemer, and she has learned to work it to perfection."

However, there was no insincerity underlying Elinor's apparent interest in Heaton's work. Her quick, restless mind loved to wander from one subject to another, and she entered into this hobby and that of her different friends with an interest which was as real as it was swift and changing. She talked politics and theology with elderly men just as eagerly as she discussed literature with Heaton, music with Wyckoff, or athletics with Ned; and unconsciously she impressed upon each in turn that this was her one especial interest. Small wonder that her companion of the moment found himself pouring all his pet theories into her sympathetic ear!

It was late, that evening, when the book was finished and they were ready to separate for the night. Heaton went immediately to his room and locked the door, before throwing himself down upon the sofa. That night, in the midst of Elinor's reading, a new and daring idea had suggested itself to him; and he wanted to be quiet and alone, to think it out at his leisure.

For weeks, he had been too much absorbed in himself to be in the spirit of work; but all at once the mood for writing had come back. Why not begin a novel, at last, and make a study of Elinor for his heroine? If he failed, what then? It would be a constant delight to write of her, even in the disguise of the conventional heroine, to fancy what she would say, or think, or do under all sorts of imaginary circumstances. No matter what was the result, there would be pleasure enough in the work itself. And if he should succeed? His brain throbbed at the thought.

Success would be sweet to him, as to any other young writer; but, beyond all that, there was the knowledge that he might put into the story some hint of his love which she could not fail to understand. He would change all the surroundings and conditions, he would make it too vague for others to realize; she surely could not resent it. And if she did read it and respond to it, there could have been nothing ungenerous in this method of telling her his love. That was the main point, and of that he felt sure, view the matter in whatsoever light he would. On the other hand, if she read his unspoken message and was unable to answer it, she would scarcely realize how deliberately he had tried to write it there. She would only smile a little over the absurdity, and then forget all about it once more.

All sorts of vague notions of a plot were rushing through his brain, and scenes and characters danced about in the darkness, dim and confused at first, then clearer and more orderly, until, in one supreme moment of clairvoyance, the whole idea, complete and entire, stood revealed to him. He started up and crossed the room to the table, to make a few notes, at least, before the inspiration should leave him.

For the second time in his life, the dawn found him still bending above his table, with a pile of finished sheets by his side. Before, he wrote to deaden his pain; this time, his destiny was in his work, and it was hurrying him on and yet on towards its fulfilment.

CHAPTER EIGHTEEN

DURING the next few weeks, Heaton gave himself unremittingly to his chosen task. Often his heart failed him and he despaired of success, often he was interrupted; but still he toiled on, for he felt that this was the opportunity of his life. If he failed, it should be his final attempt. If success awaited him, it might bring him so much in its train.

He realized all the difficulty of his plot, all the obstacles which stood in the way of his writing a story on so much broader lines than anything he had attempted before. And yet, in all his days of discouragement, he never swerved from his original plan. He felt sometimes that his real life was in the people of his story, and, as the days went on, even Elinor grew to seem less lifelike to him, and her picture in the pages before him took on all the semblance of vitality. It was not only when he was writing that he carried with him the consciousness of his story. He lived and moved in an atmosphere of his own, rousing himself at times to meet the friends outside, then falling back again into the silent inner life which to him was eloquent with the voices of his own people, the friends of his own creation.

Few men have worked under greater disadvantages. Again and again he looked back with gratitude to the night when Elinor had first suggested to him the use of the relief writing of the blind. The need for it was imperative now. Until the whole should be finished, the secret of the story must remain all his own, and it was necessary for him to go over his work again and again. The process was slow and tiresome. His touch lacked the acuteness of those who are born blind, and his time of study had been too short to develop it, or to perfect his knowledge of the arbitrary characters he must use. There were days when his fingers failed him altogether, when his brain refused to give any coherent response to the confused jumble of dots under his hand. And yet, all in all, it was a help to him. It might take him four hours to accomplish what a seeing man could have done in one; but nevertheless it was rendering the impossibility possible, and he was thankful for so much. To his mind, there was a certain fitness in it that Elinor's chance suggestion, made so long ago, should find its first real outcome in this work which he vaguely hoped might bring them together. He used to smile happily to himself, in his more courageous moods, as he pictured the day when he could tell her the whole story and show her how great was his indebtedness to her.

Day by day his work went on more surely than even he realized. There were hours when his characters appeared to take the story into their own hands, and to say and do all sorts of unaccountable words and deeds. There were hours when he sat motionless, with his face resting upon his clasped fingers, trying in vain to get the clue which he had lost at the sound of the summons to lunch, or of Ruth's voice outside; and there were moments when the words and sentences crowded into his brain faster than he could record them.

Now and then he stopped and deliberately read over his work from the beginning. It always caused him a mingled pain and pleasure, for while he groaned in spirit over its crudeness, its overdrawn scenes and characters, he yet was forced to admit to himself that its pages were keenly alive and human. Why should they not be? All-unconsciously he had placed there, not a picture of Elinor Tiemann, as he had intended, but of himself, Tom Heaton, in all his weakness and all his strength.

"You are always so busy now," Elinor said regretfully, one day. "I scarcely see you when I come here. You must be writing a three-volume novel, at the very least."

Heaton laughed uneasily.

" I am," he answered; " only it is to be in fifteen volumes, after Dumas."

" How delightful! Do put me in as heroine of a few of them. You promised to do it, you know, when we first met at Idlewilde."

" I am afraid I could never do you justice," he replied. " Please remember that I only deal with old women and sinful small boys."

" You might at least give me a namesake," she suggested, laughing. " That would be still better. I might not be able to recognize myself in the guise of a heroine; but my name would be unmistakable."

" Very well; how do you spell it? " he asked, entering into her mood with unexpected readiness.

" E-l-i, of course. Did n't you know that? I have had a prejudice against the other spelling, ever since I was a child. I used to accent it on the second syllable, and I always supposed it had some connection with emaciated people. But I did n't come here to talk about your work; I 'm much more interested in my own. We are going to have our final ' Elijah ' rehearsal, Friday night, with the full orchestra, and Herr Sigmaringen for his solos. Don't you and Bertha want to come down; or is it too trite? But perhaps you are too busy."

" I 'm never too busy for music," he answered.

" I always write better after I have heard something good, as if there were an inspiration in it. Besides, I am half ashamed to confess it; but I have never happened to hear ' Elijah.' "

" It is high time you had," she said, as she rose to go. " I shall look for you, and I only hope you will enjoy it as much as I always do."

Friday evening came, one of the clear December nights when the stars seem to stab the cold, still air with their sharp brilliancy. Inside the hall, the rehearsal was half over. The walls had just echoed with the wild chorus at the close of the first part of the oratorio, when the wind and the rain and the storm of human voices appear to vie with one another in the triumphal shout of *Thanks*. In the sudden hush of the intermission, Elinor, with Wyckoff at her side, made her way to her guests. Her face was pale, and her eyes shone like the stars outside.

" Is n't it glorious?" she exclaimed breathlessly. " I never go through that Rain Chorus without being completely carried away by its power. It does n't seem to make any difference how often I sing it. There is something grand in feeling that you are even a thousandth part of such music. I believe that it is more of an experience to sing in one's first oratorio than to write one's first novel."

" You 'll have to ask Tom about that, Miss

Tiemann," interposed Wyckoff. "I am getting a little used to her fine frenzy," he went on. "At first, I was afraid of insanity; but now that I find it is only chronic hysteria, I no longer worry. I have given up trying to get a word out of her, when once the music begins."

"Mr. Wyckoff has benevolently changed places with my flatting neighbor," Elinor explained. "But truly, don't you envy me?" she asked, turning again to Heaton, whose nerves were still quivering with the excitement of the stormy scenes on Carmel, heard for the first time.

"There's a chance for you to make a graceful speech, Tom," his cousin suggested. "Why not say that you envy me for my position in the chorus? Bertha, I shall be thankful when this thing is over. If it were to continue very long, Miss Tiemann's nervous system would be completely shattered."

"It is too bad to laugh at me," she protested. "Remember that I am a crude Westerner, unused to this sort of thing. I shall take it more calmly, another time; though I doubt if any other oratorio can ever be as enjoyable to me as this one."

"Wait till you sing as soloist in one," said Wyckoff teasingly.

"Hush," she said, as her color came. "Arturo is over there in the corner, and I don't want him to hear you. He has absolutely no sense of humor, and he would think I was really aiming at that eminence. He was politely sarcastic, at my last lesson, and he told me that I would have a very pretty little voice in time, if I were careful of it. He is glaring at me now, and I must bow to him. Behold my meekness!" And she gave a deprecating salute in his direction.

"Elinor, I am positively ashamed of your lack of spirit," said Mrs. Emerson, laughing. "The idea of being afraid of such a pigmy!"

"Though he be but little, he is fierce," responded Elinor, as the baton sounded and she turned to go back to her place. "He never grew up to fit his temper, and it has become wrinkled from being packed into such small compass."

Perhaps the second part of the "Elijah" is not quite so powerful as the first; perhaps, after his long day's work, Heaton was a little tired of listening. In any case, he found it impossible to lose himself in the music so completely as he had done before the intermission. He was only conscious that, sitting somewhere in the great chorus before him, Elinor and Jack were side by side and carried along in the same tide of musical excitement, enjoying the composer's masterpiece as only those can do who have a share, however slight, in its interpretation. It was only at the very last, when the orchestra changed to the final *maestoso*, and the chorus took up the stately movement of "Then shall your Light Break forth as the Light of Morning Breaketh," that once more the rest of the world stood remote. Then once again he sat, as if alone, enjoying the great volume of harmony which rose and swelled around and above him into the grand resonance of the final *Amen*.

All that night, the sound was in his ears. Long years before, at Idlewilde, he had lain in his hammock under the trees and listened to the choir boys, up in the cabin on the hill. They had been singing that same grand chorus. He had not known it then; now he recalled it so vividly. He could not sleep; he was content to lie passive and listen to that promise of light. It was as if past and present had met, and were sending him the same message. Involuntarily he connected it with his half-finished novel, and he fell asleep at last, resting in the hope that his light would come to him through his work, that his new day would break when once his story could be placed in Elinor's hands.

The hope remained with him all the next day, and increased until it amounted to a superstition. As he bent over his table, the words were still ringing in his ears, and inspiring him to renewed efforts. There was a sparkle and life in his work, that morning, which he had never gained before. He could scarcely believe his ears, when he heard little Ruth come toiling up the stairs to call him to lunch.

"You look tired, Tom," urged Mrs. Emerson, as she saw him make a move towards the stairs, an hour later. "Why do you work any longer, to-day?"

"I am feeling just like it," he answered. "Let me have two or three hours more to myself. Then I will be more sociable."

"Who ever expected to see you so absorbed again?" she said, as she stood looking up at him. "You were so long without writing that I was afraid you would never touch it any more."

"No danger of that," he replied, laughing. "A longing for literary success is like malaria; once get it thoroughly into your system, and there is no getting it out again. I shall probably go on writing till the end of the chapter —which will be at about five o'clock."

But at half-past four, he was roused by hearing Elinor's voice, down-stairs.

"Yes, it was too fine a day to stay in the house, so I thought I would run over to spend an hour and drink a social cup of tea with you. How did you and Mr. Heaton enjoy yourselves, last night?"

He had been on the point of making one of the most carefully studied effects of his story;

but, at the sound of her voice, it fled from his mind. He waited in vain for a moment or two, hoping that it would come back to him. Then he rose impatiently and went down to the library.

Elinor was chattering to Mrs. Emerson about some plan she was making for the holidays. As Heaton came into the room, she instantly rose to meet him, with the little air of cordiality which invariably marked her treatment of him, as differing from her manner to other men. Then the talk went rambling on to one subject after another, while the tray was brought in, and Mrs. Emerson made the tea which always adds a flavor of sociability to the most formal of conversations.

At length Elinor left them. Heaton, eager for his work again, turned away and went up to his room. As he felt for the knob of the door, to his surprise he found that the door was wide open. A moment later, a childish voice fell on his ears, —

"Hullo, Uncle Tom! I comed up here to see you, and I fought you would n't ever come back. I wanted you to tell me a story. And I 'm so sorry; but I tipped over all that great pile of papers on your desk. I put it back; but I should n't wonder if 'twas some mixed up."

Heaton crossed the room and put out his hand in search of the orderly pile of manuscript he had left when he went down-stairs. In its place, he found a rough, untidy heap of paper, piled in confusion across the whole end of the table. Ruth watched him intently.

"Uncle Tom, are you cross to me?" she asked, after the silence had lasted for a minute.

"Cross, baby? No; I hope not. Why?"

"'Cause I mixed it all up," she said penitently.

"No, baby." And there was in his tone an utter weariness which even her young ears could realize. "Uncle is used to having things mixed up; but perhaps, if he tries very hard, he can straighten them out a little. We can only wait to see."

CHAPTER NINETEEN

" My aunt, Mrs. Mackie, has just dropped down upon me very unexpectedly," Elinor wrote. " She is only to be here for a day or two ; but I want you and your brother to meet her. If you have no other engagement, go with us to Mr. Oertzen's recital, this afternoon, and then dine with us afterwards."

" You see," she explained to her aunt, after she had dispatched a messenger with her note ; " I am serving a double purpose in this invitation. I want you to meet Bertha, of course, and I suppose you will enjoy seeing Mr. Heaton again. Moreover, I have accepted so much from them, socially speaking, that it is a positive relief to be able to entertain them under proper chaperonage. It seems very good to be conventional and have a duenna once more."

Mrs. Mackie smiled, as she sat looking up at her pretty niece. She had studied the girl closely, since her arrival, the night before ; and the result of her scrutiny was satisfactory. Elinor was well, happy in her work, and developing beyond her highest aspirations. It had not been altogether with the approval of Mrs. Mackie that Elinor had taken up this life of homeless study in New York. A thoroughly domestic existence would have been more her choice for her niece than a possible musical career, however brilliant. Nevertheless, she had watched Elinor from her childhood, and she had seen the slow, steady growth of her talent and with it the restless longing for a broader training than their little western town could give. With a certain reluctance, she had consented to Elinor's coming to New York, and she had missed the bright companionship which had transformed her childless home. Now, however, she acknowledged to herself that the experiment had been an undoubted success.

It was the morning for Elinor's lesson, and the girl insisted that Mrs. Mackie should go with her. On their return, they found awaiting them a note from Mrs. Emerson to say that her carriage would take them all down town together.

"I shall be glad to meet Mrs. Emerson, Elinor," Mrs. Mackie said, as she took off her bonnet. "Your letters are full of her, and I feel rather as if she were temporarily matronizing you."

"What about Mr. Heaton?" Elinor inquired. "Don't you want to meet him again, Auntie?"

"I'm not sure."

" What do you mean?" Elinor turned to her a little sharply. " I thought you always liked him."

Mrs. Mackie raised her eyebrows at her own reflection in the mirror.

" I did like him, and all the more I dislike to see him now. He was such an alert, independent man that I half dread to see the change in him. You wrote me you felt something the same thing, yourself, Elinor, when you first came here."

" Yes," answered the girl thoughtfully; " I know; but that was long ago, before I was used to him. Now I find it hard to realize that he was ever — like the rest of us. I think you'll see what I mean. Bertha wants us to dine with her, to-morrow night, and meet Mr. Wyckoff," she added.

Mrs. Mackie waited with some impatience for the afternoon. It was not easy for her to understand the precise relation between her niece and Heaton. Elinor's frequent mention of him in her letters could not fail to make her uneasy. Three years before, she would have consented gladly to Heaton as a prospective nephew; but she could hardly be expected to approve of Elinor's falling in love with a blind man, however fine his character might be. Study as she would, she could not quite read Elinor's mind in regard to him. She must wait to see them together.

She met with a distinct shock, when the carriage stopped at the door and she stepped into it. Was this Heaton, this saddened, worn-looking man, with the hair grown white about his thin face, and the slow, uncertain motions? He met her cordially, and as his face lighted, she could see something that reminded her of their old companion of a summer day; but the likeness was faint and blurred. She watched the off-hand way in which Elinor greeted him and dropped into the seat at his side. There was no trace of self-consciousness in the girl's manner, and Mrs. Mackie's fears were somewhat allayed.

As they left the carriage and were crossing the pavement, Mrs. Mackie stopped abruptly.

"I have left my fan in the carriage," she said. "I am sorry to keep you waiting, but I shall be so much more comfortable if I have it."

Mrs. Emerson turned back with her, and Elinor and Heaton were left standing alone at the entrance to the hall. They were just in the path of the people who were passing in, and one or two of them jostled against Heaton. Elinor laid her hand on his arm.

"Come," she said; "we'll go inside the doorway and wait for them there."

The steps were strange to him, and Heaton went up them slowly, feeling his way with his feet. Inside the doorway, they halted to wait for the others.

"I feel as if I had gone backward, a few years," Heaton said, breaking the pause. "Your aunt is so exactly as she used to be that I can't realize it is more than three years since I saw her."

"Auntie does n't change at all," Elinor answered, as she bowed to a passing acquaintance. "She 's a little grayer, that is all. You don't know how astonished I was when she descended upon me, last night."

"You did n't know she was coming?"

"Not in the least. I think she took me by surprise, to see if she could catch me in mischief. She has never really approved of my studying music, you know; she always has felt that it was incompatible with my becoming a good housekeeper."

"Is it?"

"Of course not. I don't see why a woman can't bake bread and brew beer successfully, even if she is an artist. Not that I ever expect to be one. Fate was good to me, last night, though."

"You were n't in mischief, then?" Heaton queried absently.

"I was a picture of domestic quiet. My piano was closed, my music put away, and I was darning stockings. I could n't have arranged it better, if I had known what was in store for me. Even Auntie had to admit that the demoralizations of city life had left me unscathed. Here they come at last," she added, as Mrs. Mackie appeared at the foot of the steps.

Then she hesitated. When they left the carriage, Mrs. Emerson had taken her brother's arm to guide him into the strange hall. Now, as they stood together, it was natural for Elinor and Heaton to lead the way, and she was at a loss what to do. Unused as she was to leading him, she felt the embarrassment of the situation, and she shrank from the task; yet she feared that it would be too open a reminder of his helplessness if she deliberately waited for his sister to come to him. She stood for a moment, irresolute. Then, as she raised her eyes, she saw the color coming and going in his cheeks. Evidently he realized the position and found it a galling one. Her own color came, as she took his arm with a little air of decision.

"They are just behind us," she said. "What if we lead the way?"

It seemed to her that the aisle was endless, as she followed the usher to their seats; but there was no trace of hesitation in her manner when she took her place, drew Heaton down beside her, and then turned to speak to the friend she had chanced to find at her other hand. Mrs. Mackie and Heaton were talking together, and it left her a moment to recover herself. It had not been an easy thing for her to do. She had

many acquaintances scattered through the audience who could not have failed to notice her
when she came in; but she was willing to have
braved their gaze, as she saw the relief on
Heaton's face when once he was seated. It had
needed all his sister's urging to make him consent to accept Elinor's invitation, and the slight
uncertainty at the door had been a painful
ordeal to him. It was the first time that any
one but his sister and Jack had led him into
unfamiliar places; and it was at once a pleasure
and a pain to receive such service from Elinor.

"It is such a good programme," she said at
length, as she turned back to him; "German
songs, to start with. I always love Schumann;
don't you?"

"I was telling Mr. Heaton my great piece of
Idlewilde news," Mrs. Mackie said, as she leaned
forward to speak to her niece. "I had a letter
from Mrs. Rose, last week, and she says it is
rumored that Napoleon is to be married. Can
you fancy such a thing?"

"It is a little incongruous," Heaton observed,
with a smile. "I shall never forget the day the
man dawned upon me. It seemed to me there
was more unconscious humor about him than
any one I had ever met before."

"I prefer Arturo, myself," Elinor remarked,
in a low voice. "He is only three seats in
front of me, and I am in momentary terror of

his seeing me. He was in a detestable mood, this morning, just when I wished him to show off well. But here comes Mr. Oertzen."

There was the little stir of a large audience which is settling itself to listen to a favorite singer; there was the quick burst of applause that greeted him. Then the stillness dropped down about Heaton until it seemed to him that he could hear his pulses throbbing aloud. He never forgot the hour that followed. Sitting there, under the spell of that wonderful voice, a voice which sways one to tears at its will, he was only conscious that Elinor was beside him, sharing his mood, heedful of his comfort. Other people were present, of course; but for him they had no existence. He and Elinor were there together, and the songs were intended for their ears alone.

Involuntarily and without losing a note of the programme, his brain was occupying itself with the questions which, day by day, were absorbing more and more of his thoughts. She had been quick, when they stood together at the door, to read his mood and to see the passing annoyance of his helplessness. Could she have been so prompt to understand him, if she were altogether indifferent to his love? He could still feel the firm, quiet pressure of her hand upon his arm. Was her gracious act one of mere friendship alone? Had there not been some deeper feeling which helped her to interpret his thought so readily? A burst of applause roused him, as the singer left the stage for the intermission.

"No need to ask if you are enjoying it," Elinor said lightly, under cover of the murmur which sprang up about them. "I've been watching your face, and I know you like him. I'm so glad, for he is one of my favorite tenors."

"You have an unfair advantage of me," he answered a little sadly. "I shall have to assume a look of stolid unconcern. What comes next?"

"A suite by MacCunn."

"I don't know him."

"He is a new man on the programmes, and I don't know these songs at all. He is sure to be interesting, though, and with such a voice I could enjoy even Claribel," Elinor answered.

Heaton smiled at her enthusiasm.

"I had a friend," he remarked; "who went to sleep and snored audibly in 'Die Meistersinger.' It isn't safe to predict what one will enjoy. There is one thing I like about this man; he pronounces his words clearly enough so that I don't need a libretto. That makes a difference to me, nowadays," he added, as a slight sensation around him warned him that the singer had come forward once more.

With barely an introductory chord, he began to sing, and both Heaton and Elinor started into quick attention at the dainty little song which followed. Changing from key to key, varying its time and its rhythm, it was impossible to separate the words and the melody, so closely were they blended. Softly and sadly the words fell on their ears, and all at once Heaton stirred uneasily.

> " That the gloomy form of a cruel fate
>   Passed scathless through the guard,
>   And shadowed all the orient sky,
>   And smote the spring with a bitter cry."

It was like the echo of his own thoughts, which had been busy, during all the early part of the programme, with the barrier which had risen between Elinor and himself.

> " I prayed in tears, ' O, my Love, remain,
>   My Love, — my Life, my Light ! '
>   Through tears she said, ' I will come again
>   When again the skies are bright.' "

He moved impatiently, and drew his hand across his mustache. He wondered what was the use of singing such stuff. In spite of his expressive voice, the fellow could have no notion of what it really meant. It was all training, that was all. He was foolish to have it affect him so.

"Did n't I tell you it would be good?" Elinor's voice said in his ear, at the end of the next number. "It is so unusual, and so powerful."

What did she know about it? But he steadied himself to listen again, determined to hold himself aloof from the spell the singer was throwing about him.

After the quiet happiness of the second number, he was little prepared for the passionate outburst that followed. It was as if the poet and composer had looked deep into his heart of hearts and had written it all down, all the disappointment and unrest, all the throbbing passion of the man, and now he must sit there, motionless and calm, with Elinor at his side, and listen to it, and make no sign that he was writhing with the pain of it all.

> "I cry over lands and the sea,
> 'Slow the hours pass on,'
> The hours that divide me from thee,
> Will they never be gone?
> O pitiful Fates, let the night
> To the day give place,
> And the sun shine forth with the light
> Of my Love's dear face."

He drew in his breath hard, and shut his teeth together to steady his lips, while his fingers clutched the useless programme which the usher had thrust into his hand. He forced himself to think of something else, of anything which could break the strain. He tried to fancy just how sleek and smiling the singer probably looked, how well his coat fitted him.

It was of no use. The haunting, plaintive melody was all about him, and he was powerless to disregard it.

Then he had a moment's respite. The motive changed, and the pleading, restless theme died away, to be followed by a strain of utter sadness which held the audience spellbound, yet had no power over him. He breathed freer. The next moment, the words forced themselves upon his attention again, relentless and piercing: —

> " In vain my strainèd sight
>   Doth search a ray of light,
>   And now I sit in gloom appalling,
>   With lessening hope for comfort calling,
>   While on my heart despair is falling
>   Like a winter's night."

It was like the requiem of his hopes. He felt as if Elinor were slipping away from him, out into the measureless, unbroken dark, and he were powerless to grasp her. He heard nothing of the outburst of jubilant happiness that followed. White to the lips and with quivering nerves, he sat motionless, trying to conceal the pain which was overpowering him. It was cruel, cruel to bring him here to have his thoughts laid bare in any such way as this. He was roused by hearing his sister's laughing voice.

"Come, Tom, are you in a trance? I think it is time we were moving."

Elinor's face was rapt with her enjoyment.

"Was n't it wonderful?" she said. "I never heard him sing better."

Heaton's lip curved.

"His Schumann was good; but I did n't see anything wonderful in that last suite," he said coldly. "It seemed to me sentimental and over-strained; but perhaps it did n't suit my mood, to-day."

But he turned away his face to escape her disappointed eyes.

CHAPTER TWENTY

AT last it was done. The holidays had come and gone, and Easter was close at hand. All through the long winter, Heaton had worked on amid alternations of gloomy despair and fierce hope. The last light of a stormy March day was fading from his room as he wrote the final words. Then he bowed his head on his hands and sat motionless, how long he never knew.

At length he started up again, smoothed the pile of manuscript on the table before him, and locked it away in a drawer, safe from prying eyes. He let it lie there for a month. Now that the strain of writing it was over, he distrusted his efforts. His sense of the ridiculous was beginning to assert itself once more, and he almost feared to read over what he had written, lest he should find it beneath contempt.

Night after night, he resolved to take it out and read it, before another day was ended; night after night, he went to bed, leaving it still untouched. Unknown to himself, he was exhausted by the long task, and physically and mentally unable to judge of the quality of his work. He was content to drift on from hour to hour, enjoying his old quiet life by the fireside. He had not seen Elinor since the book was completed; and, for the time being, he had almost ceased to think of her. It was a relief to forget her, for a while; but this could not last. The old struggle and the old hope were bound to reassert themselves.

Elinor came to dinner, one day in late April. She had never seemed brighter nor more attractive to them all. The past winter appeared to have ripened her character from a girl to that of a woman, and her beauty was keeping pace with it. Mr. Emerson and his wife felt the change as well as Heaton, and, like him, they were at a loss to understand it. It was still early when she went away; and Heaton, after lingering irresolutely in the hall for a moment, went slowly up to his room and unlocked the drawer where his manuscript lay.

It was long past midnight when he finished reading. Even then, he made no motion to rise from the table. As if the story had been the work of another man, he had been held and carried along by its power, and its spell was still upon him. It was crude and overdrawn in places; in places it rose to greatness. All in all he told himself that it was good, far better than he had supposed. It

should try its fate. He would go back to his
old typewriter, make the best copy of the manuscript that he could, and then put it into his
sister's hands for the final revision.

It was strange that, from the first, he had
thought of no public save the publisher who
should accept it, and Elinor who should read
it. It would have to come under the eyes of
others, of course; but its message was for her
alone. What mattered the opinion of any one
else?

For the next three or four weeks, he worked
unceasingly, pruning here, revising there, always
with the old enthusiasm, always with the bright
hope dancing before him, leading him on to
more earnest endeavor. She could not fail, he
told himself, to read between the lines and
understand his appeal. Perhaps, too, if it
should succeed, the little addition to his reputation might help him to win her. He did not
reason about it. He trusted to his instinct, which
told him that this was his one chance. Success
must follow such long and persistent effort.
How else did men gain their desires? Occasionally, in the intervals of his toil, he tried to
bring himself to feel that, in spite of everything,
disappointment might be awaiting him; but it
was to no purpose. He could only wait and
work and hope.

Mrs. Emerson had been out making calls, one

afternoon in May. As she came in and went up to her room, her brother met her at the head of the stairs.

"I will be down, in a minute," she said, as she stood aside to let him pass. "Are you really going to give me an hour of your company again?"

"More than that," he said, with a smile. "My work is done, ready to go into your hands, and I can rest."

Something in the suppressed exultation of his tone struck her ear.

"What is it, Tom?" she asked.

"I have finished my story," he repeated. "Come into my room, and I will show it to you. I'm afraid it will take you a good while to copy it, though, for it is longer than the others, a whole book."

"At last!" she exclaimed. "I am so glad that you have tried it, for I have been sure you could do something beyond short stories, and I have longed to have you attempt it."

"Here it is," he said briefly, as he led the way to his room and placed the manuscript in her hands. "If you feel as if you could copy it, I would rather have you do it than send it into the clutches of a stranger. There is no use in our talking over its merits. I'm blest with a rather keen sense of the ridiculous, and I am painfully conscious of its absurdity. It is absurd; but it may have lucid intervals." He forced himself to speak quietly, though his heart was beating fast, as he put his work into his sister's hands. "Just copy it, and say nothing to anybody," he added. "When it is done, you can send it down to Lockwood and Elmore, and let them see what it is good for. Most likely it will come back to me by return express; but, till then, please don't talk about it."

With a word of congratulation, Mrs. Emerson left him and hurried away to her own room, eager to begin her task. She looked at her watch. Two hours before dinner. Ruth was busy in the nursery, taking care of a large family of dolls who were passing through an epidemic of measles, and Mr. Emerson would not be at home until late. She drew a chair forward to the window and sat down to read.

In her long experience as her brother's secretary, she had become familiar with his style; but, from the first page of this new story, she saw that he had entered an entirely different field, and that he had proved himself its master. Where had he learned to read character so acutely? How had the quiet, self-contained man in his narrowing life contrived to penetrate so deeply into the mysteries of human life and thought? How, with a few swift strokes of his pen, had he thrown his characters into such bold relief?

For several chapters she read on, held by the interest of the story, yet with no idea whither it was leading her. The plot was a simple one, only the old, hackneyed study of growing love between man and maid; but invested with a new fire and intensity from its method of treatment. Where had he gained the idea for this vain, self-absorbed woman, this grandly heroic man?

At length she reached the crowning chapter of the story, when the man, in spite of his love and for the sake of it, determined to leave the woman of his choice, rather than stand in the way of her future career. As she followed him through the supreme struggle, as she saw him again and again yielding to the old temptation, the old love, only to conquer it at the last and say farewell with a smile upon his lips, she gave a low cry of pain and let the loose sheets fall from her hands. She realized it all now.

For some moments, she sat there motionless, as if stupefied by her discovery. She was overcome with pity for her brother, with shame and remorse for herself. Stupid and blind as she was, why had she never foreseen the danger which must inevitably come to one or the other of them from their constant intercourse? Instead of that, she had only helped it on. She had encouraged Elinor's visits, and had done her best to throw her into the society of her brother. It was so plain now that, in looking back over the past year, she wondered how she could have been so unconscious of it all, so at a loss to explain Heaton's moodiness, his varying manner towards Elinor. Even then, had she realized it, she might have done much to set right the wrong. As it was, she had tried to bring them into closer companionship; she had even reproached her brother for his occasional sharpness. She knew now that it was the one relief for his exhausted endurance.

And Elinor? For the moment, she hated the girl. Why had she come there to wreck her brother's happiness? Could she not content herself to have Wyckoff at her feet, without seeking to show her power over Heaton? Then Mrs. Emerson's sense of justice reasserted itself. As she looked back over the past, she could never remember a time when Elinor had seemed to trifle with Heaton, or to treat him otherwise than she would have done a brother or an intimate cousin. Women are quick to appreciate these distinctions, and Mrs. Emerson admitted to herself that Elinor had been above reproach. No; the girl was blameless.

At first she determined to go to her brother, to tell him she knew his secret at last, and to make what amends she could for her past neglect. Then she felt that she had no right to speak. Heaton was probably unaware how much of himself he had put into his story, still less aware that there was danger of her understanding the source of his inspiration. He had asked her to say nothing of the book, even to him. If she had unwittingly intruded upon his secret, at least he should never know it. Of the future of his story she could feel no doubt. For the rest, who could tell? Elinor was young and susceptible to all sorts of new influences; she might be moved by this appeal. Moreover, Heaton was rich and would one day be famous, while no woman could demand a truer, manlier husband. Perhaps all would yet be well.

Slowly the days passed away. The Emersons had gone to their country home, where May daisies were fading and the roses of June were showing their pink petals through the vivid green of the calyx. Over the household there seemed to be a little tension, as if they were waiting restlessly on the eve of some great crisis. Mr. Emerson was ignorant of the existence of the novel; Mrs. Emerson and Heaton never once alluded to it. It had been copied and sent to the publishers, who had acknowledged its receipt in a short, but courteous note. Now there was nothing to do but to wait.

Morning after morning, as the postman left

the letters, Mrs. Emerson hastily ran them over, in search of one which should bear the well-known imprint. It came at last; and, disregarding her other mail, she seized it and hurried away to find her brother.

"It has come!" she said breathlessly, as she entered the library where he was sitting.

"Read it, please."

For once, Mrs. Emerson lost her wonted quiet, as she tore the letter open and glanced at its contents.

"How good! Listen!" And she read the note aloud.

It was short and incisive, as a busy publisher's letters must be; but there was an underlying spirit of kindliness which was far better than many words. For the rest, it accepted the novel, added a few words of congratulation upon such a brilliant piece of work, and then passed on to the details of the contract, to which now they paid scant heed.

If Mrs. Emerson had expected that her brother would be dazzled by his success, or would make any demonstration of his joy, she was mistaken. He only drew a long breath, rose and took a few turns up and down the room; then he said quietly,—

"It is settled, then. I am glad."

"But hear what he says," urged his sister. "'It is a novel of remarkable promise, and cannot fail to attract attention.' Do you realize what that is, coming from the publisher himself?"

"I do realize it," he said. "I am glad, Bertha, more glad than you can know; but even now it may not amount to anything."

He had no suspicion that she was reading his inner thought. For the hour, she had forgotten everything but her brother's brilliant success; his last words reminded her how much was still at stake. She crossed over to his side and laid her head against his shoulder.

"Tom, dear," she said earnestly; "to-day is a fitting climax to all my pride in you. Remember, whatever comes, even if you have the world at your feet, your success and happiness mean more to me than to all the rest, and your disappointment, to-day, would have been almost as hard for me to bear as for you."

He bent down and rested his cheek against her hair.

"Whatever comes, Bertha, I know you 'll never fail me."

She went away to write a note to Elinor, asking her to come out to dine with them, the following day.

It seemed to her that the next day was endless; but at last she saw Elinor crossing the lawn. She met her at the door. The girl was looking unusually bright and happy, she thought.

Could she have met Mr. Emerson in town, and had he told her the great news? Mrs. Emerson led her guest to the library; then, after a moment, she excused herself and went up-stairs to her brother's door.

"Come," he said, in answer to her knock.

"Elinor is here, Tom," she said, as she entered. "She has come out to dinner. Can you go down to entertain her, for a few minutes? I have to give Mary some orders."

A moment later, Heaton entered the room. As Elinor rose to meet him, she was struck with the new light in his face, the new energy and alertness of his whole manner.

"You look as if you had heard some good news lately," she said, as she took his hand.

"I have," he answered gravely, yet with an eagerness which he could not entirely control. "May I tell you; or don't you care about my work, when you are so busy?"

"Of course I always care," she replied heartily. "I am not so selfish as that, I hope, and I like to be told happy secrets."

"This can't be a secret much longer," he said, struck by the womanly sympathy of her tone. How quick she was to feel and share his happiness! "I wanted to tell you, myself, before you heard of it, outside. The fact is, I've a novel just accepted by Lockwood and Elmore, and they say it is likely to prove a success."

"Oh, Mr. Heaton, I am so glad! Is it really true? How proud of you we all are!" There was no mistaking the joy in her voice. "Tell me all about it," she went on. "I want to know so many things: when you wrote it, and how, and all the rest of it."

And Heaton told, simply and frankly as a child, only suppressing all the part which related to herself. She listened intently, making little delighted comments from time to time. Then, when at length he paused, she said slowly, —

"I do congratulate you, Mr. Heaton, and I shall always be so glad I knew you, all the time you were writing it. Perhaps even, a little bit of me may have strayed into it, without your knowing it. I can hardly wait to see it. And now that you have told me your secret, I think I shall tell you mine, though I did n't mean to speak of it yet. I am very happy, too, for I —" she faltered a little, as if embarrassed; then she went on more steadily, "I am engaged to Mr. Wyckoff."

CHAPTER TWENTY-ONE

JACK must never know.

Over and over again he found himself repeating these words, even before he grasped their full meaning. Afterwards he had never known just how he spent that evening. He had forced himself to appear as usual, to laugh and talk with the rest; but, underneath it all, he had constantly recurred to the one thought: Jack must never know.

Swiftly and unexpectedly the blow had fallen. He had never thought of Jack. Strange to say, it hurt him much more than if it had been another man; and yet he felt no bitterness towards his cousin. Jack had always proved his most loyal friend; now was his own time to return that loyalty. For the sake of all that his cousin had been to him, he must hide his trouble under a smiling face, and go forward and make no sign.

We rarely realize the intensity of our hopes until, of a sudden, their futility is proved. It seems quite possible to bear the disappointment, until the disappointment comes. Then we find that we have never really admitted the possibility of anything but success, and the blow falls heavily, its crushing weight all unbroken.

After any mental crisis, there comes the interval of quiet exhaustion and of passive endurance. Then follows the time of reconstruction. To go from hope to hopelessness is one thing; to accept that hopelessness and mould it to the fashion of our future hopes is quite another matter.

When the first sharp pain was over, then came Heaton's hardest time. He knew that he loved Elinor as tenderly as ever; but that, in loyalty to Jack, he must try to kill out his love. It was a hard task, for it was like trying to tear away the very roots of his manhood. For more than a year, this love had been the central point, the focus of his life, and it would have been almost as easy to destroy life itself.

The time had come for his manhood to assert itself, and he showed himself strong now. If he had been weak before, in allowing himself to drift into a relation which his destiny had forbidden him to enjoy, the temptation had come so slowly and gradually that he had not seen whither he was going, until the mischief was done. Now that his dream was ended, he roused himself to the new duty and steadfastly set his face towards the future, with a quiet endurance which left little mark upon his outer life.

It had been hard for Mrs. Emerson to lay
aside her own little dream, and to congratulate
Elinor upon her engagement. Yet she admitted
to herself that no two people could be better
suited to each other than were Jack and Elinor;
that, if it had not been for her brother, she would
have rejoiced to know they had come together.
Often as she longed to do so, she never once
hinted to Heaton that she had known of his
love. He gave her no opportunity for it; and,
as the days went on, she resolved that it was
better to keep the silence unbroken.

The summer seemed unending to Heaton,
that year. Elinor came out often in June,
sometimes alone, sometimes with Jack, but
always radiant with her new happiness, always
full of her new plans. She was to spend the
summer with her aunt; then, in the early fall,
she was to go abroad for two or three years of
study. Jack had been too generous in his love
to ask her to give up her work for his sake.
He was secure in his joy, and he could afford to
wait.

Heaton always saw her when she came. There
was no change in his outward manner to her,
save for a new gentleness which had replaced
his old moods of sharpness. He sat, by the
hour, listening to the details of her doings and
her future plans, from time to time throwing in
a word of comment or suggestion, as she turned

to him for sympathy. She had given him her friendship frankly and sincerely, and he determined to accept so much and ask for no more. It hurt him sharply now; but the time might come when he would be grateful for it, glad that he had not rejected it. Accordingly, he forced himself to meet her in exactly the old way. She was conscious of no change in him; but often, after she had gone away, he went to his room, threw himself down on the familiar couch, and, burying his face in the pillows, fought the battle once more, bitterly and long, but always bravely in the end.

Then came the weary days of correcting proof, when his sister went over the novel with him, line by line, letter by letter, both of them realizing all its hidden meaning, neither of them giving a sign of the pain it was causing them. What a mockery it seemed, now that the fire had burnt itself out, and left only dull, gray ashes! They grew to hate the story, and, in spite of the kindly, hopeful letters from the publishers, they rejoiced when they could turn away from their completed task and try to forget it.

They spent August at the Shoals, that year. The Grays had written to offer them their cottage; but, to Mr. Emerson's surprise, neither his wife nor Heaton felt any wish to return to the lake, so they went to Appledore instead.

Heaton's fame had gone before him, for already his novel was widely heralded, and he found himself everywhere received with a cordial admiration which, at any other time, must have been pleasant to him.

Now, however, he dreaded the very mention of his book, for a new fear had come to him. What if, as he once had hoped, Elinor should read all he had written there, recognize the attempted portrait of herself, and understand his love? She must either receive it with indignation, or laugh him to scorn that he had been so dull, so absorbed in himself as not to see whither she was so plainly tending. As he had listened to it, that last time, he had studied it closely, to see whether he only imagined its fervor. It was all alive and on fire with his love, and it seemed to him that no true woman could be unconscious of his meaning. He writhed in spirit, as he fancied the little contemptuous smile with which she would toss aside the book.

At last it came. One day in early October, the English and American papers announced the publication of " The Unfolded Roll of Fate " by Thomas Murray Heaton; and the busy world paused long enough to take up and read the promised novel. From the first, its success was assured, and for weeks Mrs. Emerson was kept busy, replying to the congratulations of the countless friends who suddenly discovered that they always had predicted a brilliant future for the author. Heaton smiled quietly over the notes, listened to the press notices with open scorn, and took his new honors so calmly as to surprise every one but his sister, who knew that he was waiting to hear from Elinor, before he could rest.

He had promised to send her a copy of the book, as soon as it should be in his hands; and, much as he shrank from her criticism, he had faithfully kept his word. Day by day, his thoughts followed the little package across the Atlantic and on to Berlin, where she was to spend the winter studying with an old colleague of Arturo. He had allowed so many days for the book to reach her, so many for her to read it, — he could fancy just how she would cut the string, tear away the paper, and turn over the leaves to read a line here and there, before settling down to the opening chapter, — and so many more before her answer could reach him. The time had not nearly passed, when Mrs. Emerson came into the library, one morning, with some letters in her hand.

"Such a good mail!" she said. "Here's a letter from Elinor."

"From Miss Tiemann?" His color came and went quickly.

"Yes, a long one. Let me see what she

says." And she tore the envelope open and glanced at the closely-written pages. "It's all about her music and her voyage over. I'll read it to you as soon as I can make it all out. Oh, here is a letter from her to you," she added. "Shall I read it first?"

"Please do," he answered briefly.

"MY DEAR MR. HEATON, —

"Your book is here; it came just as I was finishing my letter to Bertha, and I left everything, to read it at once. It is so late now that I must hurry to catch the mail for the next steamer; but I have just finished reading it, and I promised to tell you what I thought of it.

"It is very different from any of your other work and far beyond anything else you have ever done, stronger and better sustained, and ever so much more original in its treatment. Did n't I always say you could write a good novel? Your dialogue is capital, and you have n't written a page where the interest drags; but of course everything centres in your two characters. Where did you get your ideas for them? They both are very much alive. I can't quite read the woman, but she seems to me detestably selfish. The man is grand; he reminds me a little of Jack.

"Of course, this is only hasty criticism. I shall write you again by the next steamer, after I have had time to read the book more carefully. I am too excited now to write clearly, for the end of your story has quite demoralized me. I don't often cry over a

book; but this was too much for me. That stupid,
stupid girl! Why could n't she know?

"Cordially yours,

"ELINOR TIEMANN."

His efforts had been crowned with success;
but not the success for which he had striven
and longed. His secret was still his own.

CHAPTER TWENTY-TWO

" AND how do I really look, Jack? "

" Altogether charming, madame. Do you begin to feel the spasms of stage-fright? "

" Hush! " she commanded. " This is even worse than Berlin. There were n't a dozen people there that I knew, and here there are so many. I only hope I sha'n't happen to look at any of them. I know I should break down, if I were to meet Arturo's gaze."

" Look up at the chandelier over the stage, then," counselled her husband. " It will give you just the expression that ought to go with some of your Priestess solos. But do you honestly feel shaky? Can't you have something to steady you? "

" No; I shall be all right, as soon as I hear the orchestra. How strange it seems! " She fanned herself nervously.

" You are sure you 're all here? " asked her husband anxiously. " Score and cloak and all? You want to be sure about the cloak, for that stage is horribly draughty. I remember it of old, when I was only a chorus tenor, not the husband of the star."

She smiled faintly.

"Don't be too sure that I'm not a setting star. This is my first real test, for, after all, Berlin did n't seem to me to count for half so much. There I was only somebody's pupil; here I must stand on my own merits."

"And your cloak? I'll risk the merits; but you must n't take cold."

"Bettina has it. Is n't it all strange, Jack?"

"As to which?"

"That my cherished dream should come true, and at last I should be singing here in New York; strangest of all that it should be with this very chorus where we used to sing together."

"I wish that the 'Elijah' had come first," her husband said, while he paced restlessly up and down the room.

"Oh, Jack, why? This is so much more of a part. 'Arminius' is my best work."

"Yes, I know; only 'Elijah' was our first oratorio together, little woman. I'd have liked your début to have been in that, and leave this over till Thursday night."

She smiled up into his happy, handsome face.

"What a sentimental boy you are, Jack! At least, the fiery horses can't drag us apart now."

"I wish we had some of their caloric here, to toast you up a little," he answered, as he

took her hands into his. "This dressing-room
is no place for you. I wonder if that confounded
chorus will never get fixed."

Suddenly she started up.

"Listen, Jack! There go the violins!"

"And, by Jove, here's Edwin! I thought he
would n't miss coming in to see you, after the
note I sent him."

Three years and more had passed away since
Elinor had left New York; and now at last,
as she had said, her dream had come true. She
was to make her first public appearance in
America upon the same stage and with the
same chorus where she and her husband had
sung together, in the early days of their acquaintance. The years had ripened the girl
into the perfection of womanly beauty, until
now, at twenty-seven, Elinor Wyckoff had more
than fulfilled the promise of her maidenhood.

For two years, she had worked on alone in
the busy solitude of the great foreign city, man-
fully fighting her way onward through drudgery
and discouragement, cheered and strengthened
by Jack's frequent letters, his unswerving faith
in her future, and his generous patience in
waiting until her work was done. From the
time of her going abroad, there had seemed to
be little question of her final success. Even
Arturo had said that her voice and method
would be perfect; and at length she was gain-

ing something of that sympathetic quality which she had always lacked before. Perhaps it was coming with her natural growth towards womanhood; perhaps it came from the love that had filled her soul with a happiness of which she had never dreamed till then.

At the end of the second year, Wyckoff could wait no longer.

"Come home for the summer," he wrote. "Then, if you really must go back, we will be married in September, and I'll go over and spend the year with you. My practice can stand being left; and, even if it could n't, better lose a little, now and then, than have to spend the best years of my life away from you. Come home, dear, and let me go back with you."

And Elinor came.

The summer had been too short for the accomplishment of her many plans; but, before they sailed from New York, she and Jack spent a few days with the Emersons. Their pleasant home seemed quite unchanged to her, as she sat by the familiar fire, the night of her arrival. Mrs. Emerson had grown a little more matronly, as befitted the mother of a Harvard junior, and Ruth had left her babyhood far behind. Mr. Emerson was quite his old self, and Heaton greeted her with the brotherly cordiality which she had known so well in former days. He too appeared unchanged; his hair was a little whiter, perhaps, and he was more quiet; but that was all.

Of his work he inclined to say but little, and it was not until she was alone with Mrs. Emerson, after dinner, that Elinor learned the glory which had come to her old friend. "The Unfolded Roll of Fate" had made his reputation; but the novel that followed it had won him a place in the hearts of the people such as is granted to but few writers. The reading world was ready to lie at his feet; but he turned aside and went quietly on his way, unspoiled by flattery and adulation, as he had been by waiting and by bitter disappointment. There had been no constraint in his meeting with Elinor. On her side, there could be none; and he had forced himself to put away the memory of the last year they had spent together, and to give her the blithe greeting which befitted her bridehood.

Then the Wyckoffs had sailed away again, and, for one more year, Elinor had worked on towards the fulfilment of all her hopes. But now the years of study were ended, and at length she was to taste the sweetness of success. There had been one small recital in Berlin when a few critics had gone away enthusiastic over the young American; there had been one concert when the opera house had rung with wild applause. Then she and her proud husband had sailed for America. New York was to have a festival of oratorio; and there, in her favorite part of the Priestess in "Arminius," Elinor was to make her American début, through the influence of Arturo, who had never lost interest in his old-time pupil.

It had seemed so strange to her to be waiting in the state dressing-room, that night, while her old friends of the chorus slowly filed on to the stage and took their seats, that she was relieved when Mr. Emerson's genial face appeared at the door.

"May I come in and make my best bow?" he asked, as he crossed the threshold. Then he fell back and struck an attitude of awe. "Ye immortal gods and the nine muses! Can this resplendent mortal be my little Cousin Elinor?"

"The very one," she answered, holding out her hand. "I'm still the same old girl, in spite of my fine feathers, and I am delighted to see my dear old cousin."

"And your dear old cousin returns the compliment," he responded, as he stared approvingly at her trailing white silk gown and the close circlet of diamonds that blazed at her throat. "You are certainly good to look at, Elinor; and they say you are good to hear. Best of all, I can't see why you are n't the same Elinor, in spite of all the nonsensical raving about you in the papers."

She laughed a little nervously.

"Yes, I'm the same Elinor Wyckoff, though they did try to have me take an Italian name. I only hope I can sing so that I sha'n't disgrace you all, as I did at your house, long ago. I must go on, in a minute; but I shall see you again. Did you get the box I ordered for you?"

"Yes. Bertha and Tom are there now, with the Mackies; but I wanted to see you first. You're both of you coming to lunch, to-morrow, Bertha says."

"Jack thinks he must keep a business engagement; but I shall be there. Tell Bertha I shall look for her in the box," she added, as a knock on the dressing-room door warned her that her hour had come.

She hurriedly took leave of Mr. Emerson. Then, as he left them alone, she turned impulsively to her husband.

"I am going on now, Jack," she said, looking up into his eyes. "I will do the best that is in me, for your sake."

Her heart beat fast as she walked slowly across the front of the stage and took her seat, under the gaze of hundreds of opera glasses and thousands of pairs of human eyes. She was dimly conscious of the close ranks of the chorus back of her, of the great sea of faces before her. She knew that the tenor had bent forward to make some whispered comment in her ear, and she tried to answer him coherently. For a moment, everything turned dark before her eyes, while she heard the loud, abrupt chords of the orchestra and the first low tones of the chorus. The familiar strains brought back something of her self-control, and she turned a little in her chair. As she did so, her glance fell upon her husband, who stood at the side of the stage, watching her intently. Their eyes met, and his smile gave her courage.

The chorus was singing gloriously, and the orchestra seemed inspired. The music, rugged as the warring tribes themselves, was throwing its spell over her and filling her whole being. The crowded hall, and New York, and the modern world had fled from her, and she stood, the Priestess in the sacred grove, listening to the mighty song of the free-born sons of Wodan, watching the ruthless on-coming of the Roman legion. She knew that the moment for her first solo was at hand; but she had ceased to dread it.

As she rose, she gave one quick glance towards the middle box, where her friends sat waiting to hear her voice. She could see them plainly, her aunt and uncle with the Emersons in the foreground, Heaton a little farther back. He was bending forward in his chair, with his face turned expectantly towards the stage, and something in the intensity of his expression caught and held her wandering gaze. During the long introduction, she stood motionless; then, with her eyes still fixed upon him, she began to sing,—

> "Through the grove a sound of warning
> Stirs the mystic boughs."

Low and monotonous as were the notes, a quick thrill of pleasure passed throughout the audience. Rich and full and velvet-like, the voice held them under its sway. Then it rose to a clearer, higher note,—

> "Peace on you, oh, faithful sons of Wodan;
> Give your mourning people peace,
> Lightning-crownèd God!
> Wodan, humbly we adore thee,
> We wait for a sign from thee,
> I, thy Priestess, call thee!"

Not a motion broke the utter stillness of the vast audience, as the voice, prayerful, powerful, reverent, died away, and the chorus, almost in whispers, took up the theme; but Elinor's eyes were still upon Heaton, and she had seen his hands stiffen as they clutched his programme, his chest rise and fall sharply while he listened to her prayer.

Jack seized her hand, as she left the stage for the intermission which followed the second part of the oratorio.

"By Jove, Elinor, you never did anything to equal that consecration scene!" he exclaimed breathlessly. "Your aria was fine; but the prayer was beyond it all."

"Was it good?" she asked, dropping into a chair, while Bettina wrapped her cloak around her.

"Good! Did n't you hear them?"

"N-no; not really. I was watching Tom Heaton, and wondering what he thought of it."

"Poor old Tom! I wish he could see you, to-night, Elinor." And Jack's face softened, as it always did at the mention of his cousin.

"He can hear me," she said a little wearily.

"That 's true, and it counts for more, to-night, than ever before. You 've scored a complete success, Elinor; and the audience is all for you. I was afraid at first that it was going to be cold; but you can do whatever you like with it now."

She turned to look at him as he tramped up and down the little room, his face beaming with his pride in her.

"If you are only satisfied, Jack! You and Arturo are my most dreaded critics. But wait till my Battle Aria. That will make or mar my success."

A hearty burst of applause met her when she went out to take her place on the stage once more. During the intermission, there had been but one theme on everybody's lips, the new star that had swept above the musical horizon. Critics were exchanging golden opinions, and Arturo was surrounded with newspaper men, all clamoring for some verdict from the old-time teacher of Elinor Wyckoff. Up in the middle box above, four eager, excited people were all talking at once, while Heaton sat alone in a corner, his head resting on his hand and his lower lip caught between his teeth. For the moment, no one thought of him, and he was glad that it was so. It gave him time to steady himself, to think of the meeting on the morrow, and of the many, many meetings of former years.

Motionless, he sat there during all the next part of the oratorio. He heard vaguely and as in a dream the grand bass obligato, the call to arms; but he never stirred until Elinor's voice once more fell upon his ears. Then he raised his head, held it higher and higher as she passed from her broken recitative to the full power of her great aria, —

"Wodan! Mighty one, Lord of battles!
 From the sacred recess of thy shrine
 Guide thou the snow-white steeds, the boders of
     vict'ry!
 Haste, oh, haste thee to bring thy children succor!"

Swiftly breathless, imperious yet beseeching, the voice rang out till the air around him vibrated with its throbbing passion. It was Elinor's voice, the voice he had formerly known so well. Under its spell, he forgot his weakness, his blindness, even; its warlike fervor possessed him, and all-unconsciously he threw back his shoulders and filled his chest with the deep, full breath of a strong man who knew not the fear of darkness. It was Elinor, Elinor Tiemann before him, calling on him to rise up and conquer the Romans, and the world, and fate itself. The very air was electric with the resonance of her voice, the dramatic fire of her personality. He could feel it thrilling through and through the huge audience before him, and his nerves were tingling with its power.

"Wodan! Mighty one, Lord of battles!
  Haste, oh haste, mighty Wodan, bring us succor!"

In vain the chorus and the orchestra went crashing into the mighty war song that followed. No one heeded them, and they could only stop short and join in the general tumult. It came in waves, rising and falling, now jarring the very walls, now dying down, only to swell out louder than before, while the air was filled with fluttering handkerchiefs and falling rose-leaves. The début of Elinor Wyckoff was an assured success, and her husband's heart throbbed with pleasure as he watched her.

But when the storm had spent itself, and the leader of the chorus had once more raised his baton, she turned to look up into the middle box. Heaton had come forward into the light, and, as he impatiently drew his fingers across his lashes, she saw upon them something that glittered as sharply as the diamonds at her own throat.

CHAPTER TWENTY-THREE

QUITE regardless of the fact that "Arminius" was only the opening concert of a four-days festival, the critics of the morning papers lavished upon Elinor Wyckoff all the adjectives of their own language and even dropped into French in their fervor. Late on the morning after the oratorio, she came into their private breakfast-room, to find her husband in a sea of papers, with a pile of long clippings laid ready beside her plate. He looked up, as she entered.

"The birds are all piping in unison, this morning, madame. There appear to have been neither chorus, nor orchestra, nor any other soloists, last night; nothing but a new singer, named Wyckoff. Such notices used to make me furious, when I was one of the ignored chorus; but now I don't seem to care."

She laughed, as she bent over to give him his good-morning kiss; then she sat down and gathered the clippings into her lap.

"How silly they are, Jack! There's not a word of real criticism in them. They lost their heads entirely; and I'd rather have one word from Arturo than all this nonsense. I like the part, and I like to sing it; but that's no reason they should go mad over me."

"It was more maddening than you know, Elinor," he answered gravely. "I have heard you sing often enough; but you fairly swept me off my feet, last night. I've seen New York audiences go crazy before; but I never saw anything to equal this."

"I wonder what Arturo thought," she said musingly.

"He was parading around the wings, smiling his broadest and polishing the top of his head till it shone. I tried to get him to go in to see you; but he said he would wait till you were rested."

The waiter came into the room, just then, laden with a crowded tray. Behind him, a bell-boy brought a handful of notes and a dozen florist's boxes.

"The lion-hunters are beginning in good season," Wyckoff said, as he took them. "Isn't this from Arturo, Elinor?"

"Yes." And she tore it open. Her face flushed and the tears started into her eyes, as she read the few lines written there. "Listen, Jack! It's like a benediction on my work.

"MY DEAR MRS. WYCKOFF, —

"There was something very big and beautiful in your singing, last night, and it filled my heart full of emotion. Your success was grand; and it pleased me much, for it was like the success of one of my own children. After all my years of teaching, years of weary work when I have too often dismayed, this has given me courage to go on. I am not a young man, and my life has not been an easy one; but it is reward enough to have helped to give the world one such voice as yours. In the name of our common art, I pray you to work always to the highest limits of your soul.

"Your old master,

"MANUEL ARTURO."

Wyckoff left the room, while Elinor was still lingering over the table. He came hurrying back again, his blue eyes shining with merriment.

"Fly, Elinor, while there is time! The clerk just asked me to let him know when you were at leisure, for five reporters have been in the office, ever since six o'clock, waiting to interview you. I assured him that you were still fast asleep, and I gave the waiter an extra tip, to keep him quiet."

"What a nuisance!"

"It's one of the trials of greatness, madame. You will get used to it in time. But what will you do? See them?"

"Of course not. What time is it? Ten o'clock? Call a carriage, Jack. I'll go to Bertha's, early as it is. She will take me in, I know; and, when I am safely out of the way, you can call them in

240

to eat up the crumbs of the breakfast. You're to call for me, this afternoon, you know."

Wyckoff looked after her approvingly, as she went away. There was no suggestion of staginess in her simple tailor-made gown and her blithe manner. In spite of her dazzling success of the previous night, she was apparently as free from self-consciousness as she had been on the day of their first meeting. Proud as he was of her, his pride was nothing in comparison with his love, and he found it good that she was still the same Elinor, wife as well as artist. Life was kind to him, he told himself, and he put her into the carriage with a boyish tenderness which had its origin in their little talk over the breakfast table far more than in all the glory of the night before.

Mrs. Emerson had not expected her guest so early, and Elinor was met at the door with the assurance that she need not look for her hostess for at least another hour, as she had gone to take Mrs. Mackie for a drive.

"It's no matter," she said gayly to the maid who admitted her. "I am very early, I know; but it was more convenient for me to come now. Take my hat and coat, please; and I'll go into the library and wait. I can find something to read, and I don't mind being alone for a while."

She gave a little sigh of relief, as she entered the familiar room. In spite of herself, she felt

16

dazed by the ovation she had received, the night before. It was as if she had entered into a new existence, the intensity of which she had never imagined, even in her wildest dreams. For the moment, it was good to drop out of it, into the old life of three or four years ago. How natural the room looked! The very chairs seemed to be offering her a silent welcome from their accustomed corners. There was Mrs. Emerson's seat near the light, and Heaton's beside the fire, with her own little one opposite it. .

She moved about the room, for a few minutes, studying all the little homelike details which she remembered so distinctly. Some of the happiest hours of her life had been spent in that room. Brilliant as was the promise of her maturity, she was yet conscious of a vague, formless regret for her careless girlhood. She had paused, with her elbow resting on the back of Heaton's chair, and her eyes fixed upon the photographs on the mantel. Jack's latest one was there, and her own, and an old one of Heaton which she found it hard to recognize, so unlike it was to his present self. She roused herself from her reverie, drew a chair nearer the table, and took up the newest of the magazines that lay there.

She chanced to open to an essay which interested her; and, within a few moments, she had lost all thought of past or present. So absorbed was she that she did not hear Heaton's slow, quiet step, as he entered the room and came forward to her side. His face showed that he had not slept. Dark lines were under his eyes, and his lips were white and dry. He was thinner than of old, and he was beginning to stoop slightly, while his hair showed scarcely anything of its old bright brown. Clear as ever, in spite of their unchanging stolidity, his brown eyes were turned directly towards her while he advanced, with his hand outstretched, as if in greeting. The next instant, he stopped abruptly. Instead of the chairback for which he was groping, his fingers lay across Elinor's brow and cheek.

For a minute, his whole frame grew tense, and he made no effort to take away his hand. It seemed to him that his breath burned his throat, as he stood there motionless, waiting. He could feel the firm, warm flesh under his fingers, the curve of her cheek, the sweep of her lashes against the palm of his hand. For years, his only knowledge of her had been in the sound of her voice, the rustle of her clothing, and, now and then, the touch of her cool little fingers; yet he recognized her now by instinct. For years, he had longed to touch her face, just to freshen the dimming outlines of the old picture he had carried so long. Now at last it lay under his hand.

"Elinor!" he said huskily, and his hand dropped to his side.

In a moment it had ended. Elinor sprang up, tossed aside her magazine, and seized his hand.

"Tom! How you surprised me! How good to see you! And to have you drop formality and call me by a cousinly name at last!"

"I had no idea of finding you here," he said slowly, as he moved across to the fire.

"And I nearly made you fall over me. Here's your chair. You don't know how glad I am to see you again," she said, laughing a little in her frank pleasure. "I saw you there, last night, and I sang right straight at you. I was ever so much more interested in watching you to see how you took it than in listening to the applause from the gallery."

Heaton still stood facing her, and he shivered like a man in a chill. She saw it, and she was startled by it and by the ashy pallor of his face.

"Oh, you are ill," she exclaimed pitifully, as she drew nearer his side.

With an effort he regained control of himself.

"No; only a little tired from the excitement of last night. You have no idea how I enjoyed it all. Your dream has been fulfilled at last."

Her face lighted again, as she heard the old friendly note in his voice.

"Yes, it was more than I ever dared hope

for; but I can't make it seem real. I feel more as if I were in the dream, to-day, and I should wake up to find myself once more studying with Arturo and pouring all my ambitions into your patient ears. Those were good old days, after all." Her tone was happily reminiscent.

Heaton sat with his face turned to the fire, and his slender fingers pulling at his mustache. During the silence that followed, Elinor watched him thoughtfully, studying the change which the year had wrought in him.

"I wonder," she said abruptly, after the silence had lasted for some minutes; "I wonder if you ever remember a talk we had, one day at Idlewilde, up in the woods by the brook, when you theorized about your work."

Under his mustache, his lips straightened to a narrow line.

"Remember it? Of course. Why?"

"I appear to be in a retrospective mood, to-day," she said lightly. "I was thinking of the changes time had brought to us; that's all."

"Isn't that enough?" he asked. "The contrast is sharp, surely."

Utterly absorbed in her own idea, she went on contentedly, —

"Time has been good to us both, in some ways. Seven years ago, you were only starting

245

in your work; I had done nothing at all. We both have been successful, you even more than I."

Her voice was low and glad. It was as if she were talking half to him, half to herself, and girlishly rejoicing in her new-found happiness. Suddenly she rose and stood looking down at him.

"Life is good to us both, is n't it? We both of us have been through our dark places, now and then; but they did n't last long, and we have come through them, so they only make to-day seem all the brighter in comparison. I believe I am glad, though, that I could n't look ahead. Are n't you?"

He felt that her eyes were upon him, and he forced himself to face her with a smile.

"It 's never well to see the future too plainly," he answered. "It is likely to prove either dazzling or depressing, and both effects are demoralizing to one's work. You never would have gone through your drudgery half so steadily, if you could have seen last night's triumph."

"Nor you all the work on your first novel," she retorted; "if you had known just how it would end. You 'd have slurred over some of the most telling details. After all, though," she added more gently; "my work has been easy in comparison with yours."

Heaton's face had turned back again towards the fire.

"Yes," he said slowly; "and your success far greater."

The silence fell again. So long it was unbroken, so motionless was the man before her, that Elinor felt a nervous tension which she was at a loss to explain. For a time, she stood there waiting for him to speak. Then, obeying some sudden impulse, she stole away out of the room. A moment later, Heaton sprang to his feet and stood straining his ears to listen.

From the music-room, far at the other end of the large house, there came a strain, distant, yet distinct and vibrant with feeling. Elinor was singing the simple little "Schlummerlied" she had sung so long ago. Laden with memories, it came floating to him through the silent house, the same song, word for word, note by note, that he remembered so well; but now it was a great artist whose voice he heard, and the voice was full of the happiness of a realized golden dream.

Till the last note died away, he stood erect, with his head raised to listen. Then his shoulders shrank together and he turned away.

That night, the Wyckoffs dined with Mrs. Mackie. It was the first time for a year that Elinor had been alone with her aunt; and the two women had much to talk over, before their husbands joined them, after dinner. For a time, the conversation turned upon the events of the last few months. Then insensibly it drifted backwards, until they fell to talking of the old days at Idlewilde.

" Elinor," Mrs. Mackie said thoughtfully, as she sat watching her niece; " did you ever know how sure I was that you and Mr. Heaton would fall in love with each other?"

Half-hidden in the depths of her great chair, Elinor laughed lightly to herself.

" Why, Auntie, what an absurd idea! There was always Jack, you know."

" Yes; but before you knew Jack, all that first winter you were in New York. You were such good friends, and your letters were so full of him that I used to wonder — sometimes — " Her sentence ended vaguely.

Elinor rose and stood with one slender foot resting on the fender, and her head turned towards her aunt. Her face was very grave; but there was no self-consciousness in her voice or manner, as she said earnestly, —

" No, Auntie; it was never like that at all. I liked him better than any man I have ever seen, except Jack; and he liked me. We were good friends; he has been the truest friend to me that a woman could have had; but that was all. Tom Heaton never had any more idea of loving me than I did of loving him. There was never anybody but Jack."

CHAPTER TWENTY-FOUR

"No; I really don't dread it at all. Anybody can sing 'Elijah,' you know."

"No; it is not so at all, signora. Anybody can vocalize it; to sing it, that is quite another matter. I have heard great singers fail utterly with it. On the contrary, I have heard singers with very defectuous voices, sing it to make the tears start."

"But it is so much simpler than 'Arminius,' so much more commonplace," she urged.

"I know; but there lies the danger. Did I not tell you many thousand times in the old days, signora, that it is far more easy to sing the great things than the small? The Priestess is broad and free and dramatic. It thrills one with its passion, and makes one feel all fire and hot blood. But to sing the little *ductto* of the Widow and Elijah, that is far different. You must feel the mother love stirring in your breast as you sing. There should be no thought of the intervals nor of the expression, only of the mother love and the mother sorrow."

It was not an impressive figure who stood before her. Scarcely taller than herself, with his smooth bald head shining in the glare of the electric lights and his brows drawn together in pain at the thought of that sorrowing mother of old, Arturo stood facing his former pupil in the dressing-room, on the night which was to mark her second triumph.

Regardless of the awe which should have surrounded the idol of the hour, he had come to give her the little encouragement and admonition which he felt sure ought to help her to win another ovation. To his manifest disapproval, he had found her quite unafraid at the thought of the evening's ordeal.

"Can you not see the difference?" he went on a little impatiently. "You say the other is broader. So it may be. A priestess is greater than a homely widow; but though you may rouse the whole house to cheers with the one, with the other you can touch the heart of every single person who hears you. We may marvel at the Priestess; but we all have suffered pain as the Widow has suffered it, and as you must have suffered it, too, to sing it from the heart."

Flushed with excitement and anticipation, radiant in her happiness, Elinor took the hand of her old teacher.

"Signor Arturo," she said earnestly; "I believe you, and it is my one wish to sing so that you may be satisfied."

His face fell, and he shook his head.

"It is not that, my dear signora. Oh, why can you not see it so? You should not stop to think whether you are pleasing me, or the critics, or the man who plays the trombone, any more than you should stop to think whether it is an *F* or an *A* flat that you are taking. To sing well, you must live. You must pour into your singing all the thoughts and deeds and hopes of your lifetime, whether of joy or sorrow or of pain. In that way, if your life grows richer, so will your singing grow richer, too, and no matter how thin and worn your voice may become, there will always follow you a great, vast audience of people who are struggling and hoping, just as you yourself have struggled and hoped. It is with singing as with all art. Only by living outside your own life can you make your voice ring true."

He paused, and stood rubbing his head with his handkerchief. Then he laid his hand upon her shoulder, and looked straight into her eyes.

"They are waiting for you, signora," he said. "Go on now, and sing with all the depths of your being. I shall hear you; but you must not think of me, nor of yourself, nor of your husband, only of the music and what it speaks to your heart. Your success will be great to me, for have I not helped to make it, my child?"

Swayed by the fire of his words, she followed

him to the wings, walking like one in a dream. Wyckoff was in the box with his cousins, that night, and it was Arturo who led her to the stage door. As soon as she had crossed the threshold and come into the glare of the footlights, she was greeted with deafening applause which sent the blood leaping through her veins. Her husband's face was glowing with pride, as he watched her move slowly forward, bowing this way and that in answer to the welcoming plaudits.

There was little nervousness in her manner as she took her seat, while the conductor raised his baton and the solemn chords gave prelude to Elijah's prophecy. She heard the overture ringing out with more fire and intensity as it went on, until the coldest one in the audience caught his breath while he listened. She heard the chorus, full and glorious, rising even above the orchestra, then dying away again into broken plaint. With her eyes fixed on her score, she sat listening, enjoying it all with a curious feeling of aloofness, of irresponsibility. The audience was sympathetic from the start, she felt, yet it was as if they were holding themselves in check, waiting to reserve their fullest enthusiasm for something that was to come later.

Then the key changed, and she knew that the moment of her solo was near. As she rose, she gave one swift glance towards her husband; but

her eyes drooped again while she waited for the
few notes of the introduction. Then, in the midst
of a deep, expectant hush, she began to sing the
Widow's wonderful prayer for help.

> " Help me, man of God ! My son is sick.
> I go mourning all the day long,
> I lie down and weep at night."

Clear and sweet and true, her voice filled the
house, rising fuller and stronger as it reached
the last glad note of exultation, —

> " The soul of my son reviveth ! "

The solo was ended, and the short duet which
followed. There came a silence so short as to
be scarcely perceptible; then a quick burst of
applause, punctiliously cordial, but so cold that
it cut to her heart like a steel knife. Up in
the middle box, Jack's cheeks had turned grayish white; but, out in the wings, Arturo had
dropped into a chair and buried his round face
in his hands.

" Ah, not yet, not yet ! " he groaned. " She
has not yet lived to learn what it is to suffer."

They none of them knew how the evening
ended; but at last it was over, and Jack put his
wife into the carriage with a gentleness which
brought the quick tears to her eyes, though he
spoke no word of what had passed until they
were alone in their room together. Then he
only said, —

EACH LIFE UNFULFILLED

"Never mind, little woman. It will come, some day."

"No, Jack," she said sadly; "I am afraid it never will."

All the next morning, she shut herself into her room. Her husband had reluctantly gone away to keep an engagement, and she denied herself to every caller. Late in the morning, however, Heaton's card was brought to her door.

"Who is with him?" she asked the boy.

"Nobody, ma'am."

She hesitated. Then she said, —

"Very well. Tell him I will come, in a minute."

As she entered the great, barren parlor of the hotel, she rejoiced that he could not see the marks of the tears on her face; but her voice betrayed her, even in her few words of welcome.

"I am glad to see you," she said swiftly, as if she dared not trust her voice too far. "I have refused to see any one else; but I knew you would understand. Do you mind coming into our own sitting-room? We shall be more free from interruption there."

Arm in arm, they passed through the hall in silence. Once in her private sitting-room, Elinor led Heaton to a chair, then stood before him, waiting for him to speak.

254

"Did I do wrong to come?" he asked.

"No, oh, no; I hoped you would. I knew you understood it all, last night, and I wanted to see you then. If you had n't come, to-day, I should have sent Jack for you. It was so much for you to come here alone. I do appreciate it."

"If I could be of any use — " he began slowly.

She interrupted him wildly.

"Was n't it all cruel? I don't know why I failed. I felt it was such an utter failure; they all did, even if they are polite enough to pretend that I sang well. It is no use for me to say that I don't care, for I do. What was it? It must have been something that I could n't do, for I did all I could."

Until now, she had not given voice to her emotion. Not even to her husband had she been able to speak out; but with Heaton she let her sorrow have its way. His friendship had never failed her before; in all her girlish doubts and triumphs it had strengthened and helped her. Now was the first time in her life that she had lost confidence in her final success; and now instinctively, in her deep trouble, she turned to Heaton for sympathy. She checked herself abruptly.

"I must seem weak and childish to you," she said, with a pitiful effort at composure. "It is the first I have spoken to any one about it; but it is so hard to get used to my limitations, just when I thought I had the world at my feet. You went through it, years ago, that summer at Idlewilde, and you have lived to go on with your work, in spite of everything, and to win all you ever hoped for and dreamed of. You can help me, for you have been through it all, yourself, and come out of it, a contented, happy man."

He winced at her words. Then he rose and stood facing her.

"Elinor," he said slowly, as he drew himself to his full height; "we all of us must learn the same lesson. It isn't a question of success or failure for any of us. All we can do is to make the very most of what fate sends us, and never whine or draw back under the sharpest blows. It's a hard lesson, and we never really get to the end of it; but we have to keep on trying to work over our failures into successes, not for our own sakes, but on account of the people around us."

"Show me how, then," she said impetuously. "You have helped me before, again and again. Help me once more. I can't have Jack disappointed in me. I must succeed, after all I have worked and longed for it. Tell me how to conquer, as you did, and make something of myself, after all — for Jack's sake."

For a moment, he stood silent, his shoulders

thrown back, his head raised and his face lighted with an expression which she had never seen there before, which she was at a loss to interpret. Then he said simply, —

"I will try — for Jack's sake."

It was Elinor herself who led him to his carriage and stood looking after it, as it drove away. Already her thoughts were busy with new purposes, with the new courage and hope which Heaton had aroused within her.

But Heaton, driving away through the lonely darkness, had bowed his head on his clasped hands.

"Her dream has been fulfilled, and her success has proved to be no more perfect than my own," he muttered to himself. "And I thought I had forgotten; but— My God, how I love that woman!"

THE END

New fiction

The King's Henchman.
A Chronicle of the Sixteenth Century. Brought to light and edited by WILLIAM HENRY JOHNSON. 12mo. Cloth, extra, gilt top. $1.50.

What is more noticeable than the interest of the story itself is Mr. Johnson's intuitive insight and thorough understanding of the period. While the book is Weyman in vigorous activity, it is Dumas in its brilliant touches of romanticism. — *Boston Herald.*

Mr. Johnson has caught the spirit of the period, and has painted in Henry of Navarre a truthful and memorable historical portrait. — *The Mail and Express of New York.*

The Duenna of a Genius.
By M. E. FRANCIS (Mrs. Francis Blundell), author of "In a North Country Village," "A Daughter of the Soil," etc. 12mo. Cloth, extra, gilt top. $1.50.

An admirable novel; a pure, bright, pleasant, sparkling, wholesome, interesting story of musical taste, talent, and life. The idea is a beautiful one itself, and it is well carried out in the structure of the story. — *Literary World.*

A novel that does n't sound a hackneyed note from beginning to end. . . . One of the brightest, happiest, and most infectious of the numerous stories that have a musical basis. — *Boston Herald.*

Freshly told and charmingly conceived. Very delightful reading, and, in these hurried and high-strung days, a genuine refreshment. — *Boston Transcript.*

The Count's Snuff-Box.
A Romance of Washington and Buzzard's Bay during the War of 1812. By GEORGE R. R. RIVERS, author of "The Governor's Garden," "Captain Shays, a Populist of 1786," etc. Illustrated by Clyde O. De Land. 12mo. Cloth, gilt top. $1.50.

A well-conceived and well-told story, from which the reader will get an excellent idea of society and manners in the nation's capital nearly a century ago. — *Boston Transcript.*

Will rank as one of the successes of the year if there is any faith to be put in a capital story in a frame fashioned of our own rugged history. — *Denver Republican.*

Each Life Unfulfilled.
By ANNA CHAPIN RAY, author of "Teddy, Her Book," etc. 16mo. Cloth, extra. $1.25.

A novel of to-day, dealing with American life. Its principal characters are a young girl studying for a musical career, and an author. The scenes of the story are laid in a Western summer resort and in New York.

Hassan. A Romance of Palestine. By HENRY GILLMAN. Crown 8vo. 600 pages. Cloth, gilt top. $2.00.

The author of this powerful romance lived in Palestine for over five years, and during his residence there had unusual and peculiar advantages for seeing and knowing the people and the country, enabling him to enrich his story with local color, characteristics, and information not found in any other work of the kind on the Holy Land. The pen-portraits of the people are studies made upon the spot, and the descriptions of Jerusalem and the surrounding country are word-pictures of the land as it is to-day, and therefore of special value.

A biblical, patriarchal, pastoral spirit pervades it. Indeed, the whole book is saturated with the author's reverence for the Holy Land, its legends, traditions, glory, misery, — its romance, in a word, and its one supreme glory, the impress of the Chosen of God and of the Master who walked among them. — *The Independent.*

Mr. Gillman has certainly opened up a new field of fiction. The book is a marvel of power, acute insight, and clever manipulation of thoroughly grounded truths. There is no question that it lives and breathes. The story is as much of a giant in fiction as its hero is among men. — *Boston Herald.*

The impression made by reading the book is like that of witnessing a great play, its scenes are so vivid, its characters so real, its surrounding horizon so picturesque, its setting so rich and varied. — *Philadelphia Item.*

Sielanka: a Forest Picture, and Other Stories. By HENRYK SIENKIEWICZ, author of "Quo Vadis," "With Fire and Sword," etc. Translated from the Polish by JEREMIAH CURTIN. Uniform with the other volumes of the Library Edition of Sienkiewicz. Crown 8vo. $2.00.

This new volume by the most popular writer of the time includes the shorter stories which have not before been published in the uniform Library Edition, rendering it the only complete edition of his works in English. It comprises six hundred pages, and contains the following stories, dramas, etc. : Sielanka, a Forest Picture; For Bread; Orso; Whose Fault, a Dramatic Picture in One Act; On a Single Card, a Play in Five Acts; The Decision of Zeus; Yanko the Musician; Bartek the Victor; Across the Plains; The Diary of a Tutor in Poznan; The Lighthouse Keeper of Aspinwall; Yamyol (Angel); The Bull Fight; A Comedy of Errors; A Journey to Athens; Zola.

Under the seventeen titles one finds almost as many aspects of the genius of Sienkiewicz. Detached from the intricacies of an elaborate composition, figures, scenes, and episodes become far more effective. — *New York Times.*

In Vain. By HENRYK SIENKIEWICZ. Translated from the Polish by JEREMIAH CURTIN. 16mo. Cloth, extra, $1.25.

A love story of modern Poland, by the author of "Quo Vadis," not before translated. The scene is laid at Kieff, and university life there is described.

The Story of Gösta Berling. Translated from the Swedish of SELMA LAGERLÖF, by PAULINE BANCROFT FLACH. 12mo. Cloth, gilt. $1.75.

When "Gösta Berling" was first published in Sweden a few years ago, Miss Lagerlöf immediately rose into prominence, and, as Mr. E. Nesbit Bain writes in the October "Cosmopolis," "took the Swedish public by storm."

The sagalike treatment and almost lyric mood of "The Story of Gösta Berling" render its form in keeping with the unusual character of the book itself. The harshness of Northern manners enables Miss Lagerlöf to probe human life to its depths; and with the effect of increasing the weird power of the whole, a convincing truth to nature is intermingled with the wild legends and folk-lore of Värmland.

There is hardly a page that does not glow with strange beauty, so that the book exerts an unbroken charm from beginning to end. — *The Bookman.*

Something Homeric in its epic simplicity runs through the history of the deposed priest. The opening chapters engage the attention at once by their mystic realism. — *Time and the Hour.*

I am the King. Being the Account of some Happenings in the Life of Godfrey de Bersac, Crusader Knight. By SHEPPARD STEVENS. 16mo. Cloth, extra. $1.25.

A fresh and invigorating piece of reading. — *Nashville American.*

Characterized by those graceful touches which belong to true and pure romanticism. — *Boston Herald.*

It has the straightforwardness of the old-time story-teller. — *St. Louis Globe-Democrat.*

The Duke's Servants. A Romance. By SIDNEY HERBERT BURCHELL, author of "In the Days of King James." 12mo. Cloth, extra. $1.50.

A highly successful romance, of general interest and of creditable workmanship. — *London Athenæum.*

Pastor Naudié's Young Wife. By ÉDOUARD ROD. Translated from the French by BRADLEY GILMAN. 12mo. Cloth. $1.25.

M. Rod's new novel is a study of French Protestantism, and its scene is laid in La Rochelle and Montauban, the two Huguenot strongholds. It was first published in the "Revue des Deux Mondes," and at once achieved success. "M. Rod's work," says Edmund Gosse in the "Contemporary Review," "whether in criticism or fiction, always demands attention." "The Catholics," says a writer in "Literature," "praise the book because they find in it arguments against their adversaries; the Protestants, while protesting that the author, because he writes in the clerical *Gaulois*, is none of theirs, read it to discover personal allusions to their spiritual guides."